# Graveyard Tour

# Darren Shell

Courthouse artwork by Livingston artist, Mala Terry, © 2003

©Copyright 2008, Darren Shell
No part of this book may be reproduced, stored in a
retrieval system, or transmitted by any means, electronic,
mechanical, photocopying, recording, or otherwise,
without written permission
from the author.

ISBN: 978-1-60414-034-7 / 1-60414-034-8

# Acknowledgements

Writing this book has been an absolute joy for me. During the infancy stages of its writing, it was my intention to showcase a true *hometown* by displaying the subtle little qualities that make it what it is…a home. I intended to seek for this special hometown out there in America someplace and study it. I wanted to find out the nitty-gritty's that make life pulsate through it…make its residents love it. I wanted to find that feeling of home. I found that feeling in Livingston, Tennessee.

During my research for this book, the city of Livingston has received me with open arms. Every person I contacted or met stopped what they were doing and offered their complete assistance. All involved were enthusiastic, friendly, and fun. They happily offered that compassionate feeling of home I wanted to find and did it with ease. I offer my thanks to this city for its warm hospitality and generosity. In it, I found *home.*

I would personally like to thank my local history guru friends, Ronald Dishman and Emily Sells. You both make this town's history even richer.

A big thank you goes to Mala Terry for her artwork, friendship, and energy. She has always been an inspiration to me.

I would like to thank Mayor Curtis Hayes for his enthusiastic support of this book, seeing its potential from the beginning. Thanks for dragging me around town and introducing me to the seemingly endless stream of smiling faces and names you know by heart. You are a true *hometown* mayor.

Another thank you goes to Mickey Ledbetter and Josh Beasley for their computer know-how. Without them, this book would have been a pencil sketch.

To Mark Willis, Delores Bender, and my mother, thanks for the tireless and painstaking proof reading. You each have nerves of steel.

I would also like to express my gratitude toward the many families that have generously allowed me to write about some awkward family history. I sincerely hope I have not offended any of you. That was never my intention.

I am enormously grateful to the Roberts family, for letting me write about old Harry.

To the businesses of Livingston; Livingston Enterprise, Apple Dish, Antique Market, Dairy Queen, and others … thanks for not only allowing your establishments to be a part of this book, but for just being a part of this hometown. Keep up the good work!

And lastly, I offer my thanks to the most supportive family that a man could wish for. If they are not behind me … they are carrying me. My parents, my sister, my lovely wife, my daughter…thank you all for your loving support.

I hope that as the chapters of this book unfold, the reader can experience the same love of this little town that I have come to enjoy. I hope that feeling of home is shared by all who read this short little novel. We'll meet ghosts of Livingston's past … and share frightening stories from the days of old. But keep your flashlights handy, friends. This ain't no joy ride. You're on the *Graveyard Tour*.

This book is dedicated to the descendents and family of Harry Springs. May the Stoneman always be alive in our hearts.

Harry, Ida, Mary Lou, Mable, and Alice Springs

**"An Interview with Mr. Rich"**

February 15, 1985

"I remember it like it was yesterday. I've never been that wet before…or cold, for that matter. Some nights I awaken from startling dreams and still feel the chill from that one day of my life. Even though I became a close friend to Harry, my first meeting with him was frightful, to say the least. My sixteen year old mind aged many years that day.

It was the wee hours of the fifth of April, 1911. I had gone to stay with friends who lived near Alpine, Tennessee. Momma had let me go, just to make some money, 'cause Daddy was still somewhere on a log raft along the Cumberland. Logging had always been a part of our family from way back into the days of my grandparents. Logs would be cut here along the shores of the Obey River and bound together for a trip downstream to Celina, or maybe even as far as Carthage or Nashville. I never went that far though. Daddy had always said the river was no place for a young'un. Even the headwaters of the Obey were a rough and tumble place.

Even though Mamma and Daddy didn't want me mingling with the "river folk", we needed money—and I loved the river. I can still close my eyes and see and smell the water and trees. I can hear that old cross-cut saw dragging back and forth. The word "TIMBER" still echoes in my head, just as it did in the hollows of my youth. Yeah, it was hard work…real hard work…but I loved it. I don't think Momma ever appreciated the river like me though. She felt the river was made of moonshine and witchcraft, and she didn't want her family caught up in none of it. I don't know anything about witchcraft, but I'd be lying if I said I never took a nip of moonshine. It warms the innards, you know.

My first trip onboard a raft was a real Hell-bender. We had waited for days for rain to raise the river enough to gain enough current to begin our trek. Our logs were bound and staved, and our oars had been secured to the raft, front and back. It must have been my beginner's luck, because we got a two-inch downpour of rain, and then it turned sunny and beautiful. I rowed harder on that first trip than I ever realized I could. That quick gulley-washer had the river running top speed. Lord, I just wanted to hear the captain yell out "DO EASE!" That was the term they used to have us stop rowing. The only time we rowed was to steer. We just let the raft float with the current, but the rowing seemed almost constant in the long and winding curves of the river. We'd row one way, then the other—all day long. You wouldn't think that a fella could love that kind of work, but it just sort of gets in your blood. Lord, that was a rough few days of my life, but it got me hooked.

Oh yeah, back to the first day I met Harry.

*Graveyard Tour*

This wasn't one of those pretty days like my first trip. I was working with my friend, Jimmy, and his dad, John Winningham. All three of us had been hired on by Porter Smith and his oldest son, Illis. Those two were some hard working men. They were almost crazy with it. When the rains came, it was time to work. It didn't matter what time of day it was, we worked. Rain, shine…Hell or high water, we worked.

We knew that when the sprinkles of rain began to fall on the tin roof of Jimmy's house, that we would be up before dawn and down to the river. We had busted our tails the day before staving a particularly large raft. It wasn't tied well enough to suit Porter, and we worked on it until way past dark. The light of the lantern just wasn't enough to finish the job, so we elected to complete the raft early the next morning. Bad idea. We had not expected the rain to fall before morning. And it fell, alright. It was a real goose-drownder. I had never seen or felt rain like that ever. It could not have been much more than forty degrees, and we were all chilled to the bone. I couldn't keep the rain from my eyes long enough to tie my staves. Porter was now down right mad. He was throwing ropes and cursing left and right…even shouting at the river to stop rising. But the river listens to nobody but God, and He wins when He plays the game. I don't think none of us should have been there that day, but we were.

We were in a stretch of the river known as Taylor Island. During rains like this one, it was no island…just a shallow spot in the river. Porter and Illis were throwing lines to us, and we were trying to tie off the raft with little success. Then it happened.

Jimmy was holding tight to a line and had it wrapped around an old snag of a stump. Porter heaved another heavy rope to him to tie off. In the torrential rain, Jimmy just didn't see it coming. The coil of rope hit Jimmy square in the head. The force of the blow knocked him backward and into the cold water. He was able to scramble out of the river quickly, but that wasn't the worst of it. When he fell, he let go of the rope securing the upper end of the raft. The huge raft began to swing around in the swift current. Porter and Illis jumped up onto shore to get out of the way, but Jimmy's dad was caught up in the mud and mire further down shore. He had been waist-deep, securing a lower line. The poor man saw what was coming and frantically pulled and tugged at his feet, trying to free them from the muddy river bottom. There he stood, waist deep in the river, with a hundred logs coming downstream at him.

I raced toward him, wiping rain from my eyes. By the time the raft reached the shore, I was pulling on the old man's hand for all I was worth. But I was too late. It was awful. Even in the rain and wind, I heard his ribs break…felt his whole body give as I pulled. I thought his eyes would pop right out of his head. God, I felt bad for him.

As soon as the raft hit shore, it crumpled into pieces. It bounced as it hit, and I was able to pull Jimmy's dad from the mud and muck. He quivered and shook, as he twisted in agony in a pile on the muddy river bank. Porter was screaming and cursing at the top of his lungs, instructing us to help catch logs. But it was of no use. We knew Jimmy's dad needed help. We lifted and carted him on our shoulders toward home, over five miles away. It was an exhausting walk. I didn't think we would make it to Jimmy's, and I surely did not think his dad would survive us dragging him home. That log smashed him through and through. I can't shake that sound from my head…that pop, pop, crunch of his ribcage…makes me sick to think of it.

We pulled him up onto the porch of the house and into the one and only room the cabin had to offer. I remember how beautiful that fire in the mantle looked to me. I literally shook from head to toe with cold, and Jimmy was no better. John looked as if he may die any second. We had him laid out on the feather tick bed before Jimmy's momma knew what was happening.

As Jimmy attempted to relay the story, his momma grabbed him by the shoulders. "You gotta get Missa Springs! You gotta!"

I had no idea who Mr. Springs could be, and I think Jimmy only

*Graveyard Tour*

half-way knew. But fortunately for his father, Jimmy did know the way to the man's home, some six miles away.

Even though Jimmy was exhausted beyond belief, he never hesitated. He grabbed another coat…one drier than the one he had on…and raced out the door. He turned before he left and gave me a two-word command, "Help Momma." If those two words don't make a kid feel helpless, I don't know what could. I stood paralyzed with cold and fear, not knowing how to help, even if I could. All I wanted was that fire.

Soon, I could hear the sound of galloping hooves in the mud, and I knew that Jimmy had mounted the family horse. They rarely ever rode the old nag, being a large and cumbersome draft horse, but the sound of her hooves was a delight to my cold ears that day. I felt a little better now that I knew Jimmy could at least *ride* those many miles to Livingston.

Despite not knowing what I was doing, I quickly began pulling wet clothes from John, as he lie motionless on the bed. The man did not have enough energy to quiver. He was now unconscious, and his pulse weakened. Mrs. Winningham sobbed uncontrollably. I suspected she had the same hatred for the river that my mother possessed, and this occurrence only solidified her beliefs. I felt terrible for her, kneeling by the bed, his hand in hers as she cried.

We eventually got all the wet clothes from his body and covered him with a number of quilts. Mrs. Winningham rubbed his arms as if to move blood within them. She kissed his brow, all the while crying continuously. We sat beside him for what seemed an eternity. It must have been about midday, yet we had no idea of the time with the terrible storm raging outside. The sky grew darker and the wind increased. I wondered if I shook from cold or fear. It was a horrendous storm, and I felt helpless tucked away within the walls of this cabin…trembling as rain pelted the panes of the windows.

I imagined the sound of hooves at least a hundred times, and I made many trips to the window, hoping to catch a glimpse of Jimmy and Mr. Springs, whoever that was.

After another hour of watching rain splash the wavy glass of the window, I finally saw two figures ride up on the horse. One jumped from the horse and ran toward the house. The other (Jimmy) led the horse to the pasture. I could no longer focus on Jimmy and turned my attention to the door.

As I reached for the latch of the door, it swung open before me. A flash of lightning revealed a startling silhouette of a man at the door. A tall dark shadow dripping with rain raced past me. I jumped aside to avoid being toppled.

The wide-brimmed leather hat of the stranger still poured rain as his voice pierced the air. "What happened?"

"You gotta help him, Harry…you gotta!" Mrs. Winningham was still sobbing and in no condition to describe what little she knew of today's events. Heck, I didn't even know how to tell him.

"You gotta help him!" she cried again.

"Get aholt a yourself, woman!" he shouted back to her. "It don't work dat way, an' you know it!"

"Logs crushed him in the river…he's bleedin' bad inside, Harry…you gotta help him!"

I wondered how the old woman knew he was bleeding internally, but one look at the bed linen told the story. A pool of blood had leaked from his body, and it covered a large portion of the bed. You don't just up-and-stop a body bleeding internally. I didn't know what she wanted the poor fella to do…reach in and fix it? It was then that I got scared. I mean real scared. I'll never forget the look in that man's eyes. I'll never forget the reflection from the fire shining on his deep ebony skin. He looked like nothing I ever seen…not afore…and not since. He looked possessed.

This man, this Harry Springs, took to digging stuff out of a leather pouch he had brought with him. I had never seen the like of this stuff, either. He had strange roots and herbs with him, and he spread 'em all around the bed. I stared in disbelief, as he started chanting quietly and rocking back and forth on his haunches. "BOY!" he shouted at me. I nearly fell over. His voice might as well have been a cannon. It wouldn't have made no bigger an impression on me. My heart nearly stopped. "BOY!" he shouted again.

"Yes, sir!" I quivered.

"Where's the garlic?"

"I...I...dunno."

Mrs. Winningham pointed toward the mantle. As I looked in the direction that she was pointing, I could easily see many cloves of garlic laid out on the mantle. This seemed strange to me, but some of the black folk ways just didn't make sense to me. I never understood the blue-green paint around the doors and windows either, but it all made sense to those that lived within the walls of these homes. That special painted color kept out the "haints", or "haunts", if you will. Regardless of what spirits they wanted kept away, the spirit in front of me now was Mr. Harry Springs...and I was not about to question his actions.

"Get 'em, boy. I wants 'em in every window...every door... NOW!"

I quickly scurried away at my task. My spine was ICE-COLD. You just have no idea how dang scary that man was. Those eyes were black as coal, and it was like there wasn't no bottom to 'em. And yet, every emotion under the sun was in 'em. My God, I was scared. All I could think about was Momma and her tales of witchcraft. I thought to myself...now you've done it...done got yourself all wrapped up in the witchcraft. I wanted out of there, but I was too mesmerized to take my eyes off of what was going on. I was beside myself.

Just then, the door burst open and Jimmy jumped inside. The harsh wind from the storm followed him in, and a large clap of thunder shook the house as Jimmy knelt down by the bed. "What can I do?" he asked.

Harry grabbed him by both shoulders. "Pray Ezekiel, Boy! Pray!"

I had no idea what Harry meant by that. I understood *pray*, but that was it. I began repeating, under my breath, numerous pieces of prayers that I had heard through the years. I am sure none of it made sense. "Father, Son...Holy Ghost...hallowed be thy name. Walk with me in the valley of shadows..." I had no idea what I was saying or thinking. I was still absolutely petrified. *Witchcraft...* Momma will kill me.

"BOY!" he shouted again, and again every ounce of breath left my body. "Pray Ezekiel, BOY!"

"I...I...um...don't know..."

"Then pray for us," he commanded. "We all gonna need it." He picked up a lit candle by the bed and poured the hot wax onto his hand. His eye squinted as the wax hit his skin. He then dribbled it in a circle around the bed linen covering Mr. Winningham. His eyes were closed and he continually waved his arm across the bed as if he were wiping snow from it. From head to toe, he waved his hand over and over. All the while, he chanted this verse.

"AND WHEN I PASSED BY YOU AND SAW YOU STRUGGLING IN YOUR OWN BLOOD, I SAID TO YOU IN YOUR BLOOD...LIVE! YES, I SAID TO YOU IN YOUR BLOOD...LIVE!"

He reached over to Mrs. Winningham and wiped a tear from her cheek. He spread that tear over Mr. Winningham's forehead, still chanting and rocking back and forth.

Now I know he was chanting the Bible, chanting Ezekiel 16:6. But at the time, I was completely lost. Those words made no sense to me. I guess they are well known by faith healers the world over for their power to stop bleeding. It all sounded like witchcraft to me.

By now, I had backed myself completely against the wall. My lips were blue with cold, and my spine was numb with fear. My arms trembled by my side. But my fright was only just beginning. Harry suddenly stopped his chant, as if suddenly realizing something. His glare turned directly to me. "Who was with you, Boy?" he asked with a cold and foreboding tone in his voice.

"Mr. Smith and his son," I chattered.

His head dropped with dread. He slowly raised his head again and looked me in the eye. With a shake of his head, he said again, "Pray, Boy, Pray."

At that very second, a clap of thunder shook us like nothing I had ever felt. It was so loud and strong that it hurt every fiber of my being. The lightning that went with it illuminated the room. John's chest rose with breath to meet Harry's hand, and his eyes opened.

"I SAID TO YOU IN YOUR BLOOD...LIVE!"

Five miles away, Porter and Illis crouched beneath a cluster of trees on the riverbank, fearing for their lives. The same clap of thunder shook the hollows of the Obey River, and lightning left the sky and terminated in the trees along shore. Amid the swirling dark skies along this churning river, the Smith boys fell dead instantly."

\* \* \* \* \*

Clickety-clap. The tape recorder on the desk stopped at the end of its tape. An eager young reporter nervously rummaged through his bags for another fresh tape and spoke up. "That is a fantastic story, Mr. Rich. It gave me chills."

"It still gives me chills after all these years."

"I can't believe Mr. Springs could heal people that way." The reporter continued to rummage around, pulling everything but what he needed from his bag. "Do you suppose he killed those Smith fellows?"

"Harry Springs never killed nobody. He just balanced the scales, that's all."

"I don't think I understand, Mr. Rich."

"For Christ's sake, Boy. Ain't ya got no common sense? He wasn't no witch doctor, diggin' up bones. He just sorta helped balance things, that's all. He was a faith-healer…a self-proclaimed soothsayer. Don't nobody know what's goin' on in their head. Not nobody. It just is what it is, that's all. They didn't just make good or evil. It don't work that way. He just sorta shifted the weight of the scales. For every action, there is an equal and opposite reaction. Remember that, boy. You don't tip the scales without repercussions."

"It just seems outlandish…you know…roots, herbs, witchcraft?"

"Boy," the old man said in a harsh tone, "I didn't say it was witchcraft, I just worried that it might've been at the time. It's like this. Harry Springs was a good man…a real good man. Anybody got something to say about him, can say it to me…and face the consequences."

"I…I'm sorry," said the reporter, confused by the sudden change in the man's demeanor. "These are fantastic stories."

"Boy," said the old man, "you ain't heard the half of it."

# 2

### "Crown Jewel of a Stoneman"

With a wry smile, the enthusiastic young reporter slapped a new tape in his recorder. "I've got to hear this. Carry on, Mr. Rich."

"You orta been here in Livingston, in 1932," he said. "Old Harry caused a lot a stir. He and the extension agents always had a tussle. They were all knowledgeable men, but Harry always seemed to get the best of them. 'Course, they had studied at every college across the state and knew all the proper ways to plant crops and harvest what they'd sown. Those boys studied and did well in the field. But old Harry just carried an almanac and studied the signs."

"What signs, Sir?" asked the reporter.

"You know, the signs. Astrology…the moon and stars… Capricorn, Cancer, whatever."

*Darren Shell*

"You mean like how the almanac has all the phases of the moon?"

"Yeah...here's one of my favorites." He gave the lad in front of him a faint smile and continued. "The agents were having a demonstration day in town. They had been doing the same thing every week for the last two weeks, and Harry had been present for all of them. It was a simple session about digging in corner posts for fences. They would dig a few post holes and install cedar posts... commenting on proper installation of cross-bracing and stretching procedures. They were about to start tamping in the posts when Harry spoke up."

"Where's your wheel barrow, Johnny?" he asked.

Johnny was distracted from his tamping and replied, "I haven't needed a wheel barrow all month. The dirt here is good soil...it tamps real nice...it has all month."

"It's a new moon, Johnny," said Harry, "I can go fetch one for ya. You'll need more than one to haul away the extra dirt. Ya never fence on a new moon."

"Hogwash, Harry," said Johnny, "I been doin' this a day or two. I think I can handle my own demonstration. Thank you anyway. This here dirt will tamp real nice."

"Well, Johnny had to eat a good bit of crow that day. He nearly tamped his fingers off, but couldn't make all that dirt push back in those holes. Johnny just pushed the dirt up around the posts and stomped away."

"Barnyard Nigger done put a spell on me..." Jimmie would say. "Watch out fer 'im, boys. I don't trust him none. It's witchcraft, or I'm a monkey's uncle."

"Strange thing, though, Harry never hesitated to help. He even went over to help Johnny the next week at cuttin' briars and bramble

*Graveyard Tour*

out of a field. He said Johnny never would have enough time before the next moon to get 'em all cut. Those briars would just come back next year if you didn't cut 'em at just the right time of the moon. No sense in wastin' effort. He just up-and-helped him. He was a good fella, I'm tellin' ya. I'm not sure Johnny ever trusted him, but he sure took that help in the field. Nobody ever turned down help cuttin' briars."

"That's just the way Harry was. He was always studying the stars and signs. He could tell you the phase of the moon any day of the week. He studied the signs, that zodiac stuff. It worked into every detail of his every day. He was a special fellow."

"Most of the money he made was around town. Not doctoring and stuff, though. He never charged nothin' for that. Said that was the Lord's work."

"He made his living working in town as a stone mason. Yep, he mined the rocks right out of the mountain, up there where he lived on Rock Crusher. Him and a bunch of fellas from Celina and Cookeville would set up tents on the mountain and just carve and pry rocks out of the quarry until they had a bunch. Then they'd haul 'em all down into town and build foundations and walls and stuff with 'em. He built that wall next to that real purdy house on East Main… that one next to the flower shop. He laid all that stone in that wall by the old library too. I guess he even made up cemetery headstones. I think he just made 'em for his friends that couldn't afford the fancy, new-fangled ones. I'd rather have one of his anyway…they looked neat and rugged. He sure was a talented fella."

"Most folks don't know he did all that stonework. He had his little girl working with him too! No kiddin'! That little girl helped with all that heavy rock laying stuff. She was a tough one…sweet little thing, too. Shame she never married. Harry died when she was young. I felt somethin' terrible for her."

"Well, Mr. Rich," said the reporter, "would you like to end our interview on that?"

*Darren Shell*

"End it?" he asked defiantly. "End it? Hell, you ain't heard the best part…the crown jewel in Harry's crown. You and me are settin' here 'cause of him. Don't nobody know it, but it's so. We owe a debt of gratitude to that man, and don't nobody care. We all pull up that newspaper clipping from *The Enterprise* from way back and laugh at him. Laugh. Dang, that one boils my blood. Without Harry Springs, we wouldn't be here in this cozy house sippin' coffee and a chattin'. We are here…'cause he gave all. He absolutely gave all. And don't nobody care. Boils my blood, yes it does. We owe January of 1932 to Harry Springs, and him alone. I don't see no monuments…no plaques…not a single dad-gum picture in City Hall. His grave over in the Cash Cemetery don't look no different than nobody else's. This is beautiful downtown Livingston, Tennessee, and don't nobody know Harry Springs. That's a shame, boy…a dad-gum shame."

"Sir," commented the reporter, "I don't see how Harry Springs could have changed much in the town of Livingston. His name is not represented in any of the history books I have read. Could you be mistaken, Sir?"

"MISTAKEN? BOY! I LIVED IT! I don't need no smart aleck school boy questioning me about Harry Springs. I can end this silly interview right quick if you don't believe what I'm sayin'."

"No Sir. No Sir. I believe you. I just asked a question, that's all. You must admit…there is no mention of Harry in the history books."

"That's another dang shame, boy. This is a wonderful little town. It has all kinds of great history and stories to tell. But people should know Harry Springs. They should have watched as I did back in '32." The old man scratched his head and gave a long sigh. "But that was a long time ago. I don't suppose it'll ever be recognized for what it was. So unless you are in a hurry, I'm gonna go ahead and tell you about that night. Everybody should have seen what I saw…everybody."

*Graveyard Tour*

The young man looked down at the recorder spinning in front of him. His gaze again met the sparkling eyes of Mr. Rich. "I'm all ears!"

The old man rummaged through his pockets. "I knew you would want this eventually. I figured I might as well show it to you right off. This is how the *Livingston Enterprise* and the whole dang town saw it. They published this during that awful time. It broke Harry's heart, but it didn't really matter by then. It was done too late. Livingston never knew what he gave…what he endured for it. This is what the smart-aleck public saw and understood."

He pulled a piece of tattered paper from his pocket. He unfolded it to its full extent and handed it to the young reporter. The lad had seen it before…it was part of the reason he had chosen this particular story as his first real in-depth interview.

*The Livingston Enterprise, January 29, 1932.*

*Livingston To Be Swept From Map by Huge Storm. Negro Sooth-sayer, Harry Springs, predicts devastation and destruction in Livingston and nearby Gainesboro and Celina.*

*Harry knew because he "had talked to the Lord," and "the Lord told me so."*

*This removes him from the soothsayer class and puts him in the realm of spiritualists or some other group that commune with the "other world".*

*Winds from said storm did not "materialize", and Livingston is safe. No other fronts appear to be on the horizon in the near future, and residents should practice the least worry at this time, giving that Livingston is still on the map.*

"I was there, boy. I looked into his eyes everyday for a week, while tears fell and he worried himself about Livingston's demise. You don't just up-and-fix Mother Nature and God. They're gonna do what they're gonna do. It don't matter. But, I could see it in his eyes. I could see long before it happened what would unfold. I knew Harry well enough. I knew…he'd find a way to help."

The old man paused and took a long and deliberate breath. "I walked with him that day back in '32. We had become good friends, and he did not forbid me from coming along. He didn't like it though. He kept saying…*This is between me and God.* That scared me to high heaven. Harry was always positive…always happy, but not that day. It was a balance, I tell ya. Balance. He told me many times…*Don't go tippin' the scales, boy. It don't work that way.* I saw what happened that night, boy. I saw what the town of Livingston didn't."

The reporter nervously looked down at his recorder. There was still room for more recordings. He reassured himself with a stretch of his arms and a slight yawn. This man's story was getting deep.

"We walked from his home to the very top of Rock Crusher Mountain. There he stood in the rain, high on the bluff overlooking the city. I mean winds were a whippin' 'round. Clouds rolled in the sky. I felt like I did that day twenty years earlier when old man Winningham was saved. I had no idea what Harry had up his sleeve, but I knew if anybody in the whole world could help Livingston, it would be Harry. Just as I suspected, Harry started his chants and rocked himself back and forth in the mud and rain on the mountainside."

"The sky looked like nothing I had ever seen. It didn't surprise me. When Harry was around, strange and fantastic things happened. He made them seem almost ordinary. I guess, in comparison to him, the extraordinary seemed ordinary. I don't know. All I knew that day was that something BIG was about to happen. And happen it did."

"The storms Harry had predicted began to form in the evening sky. Huge black clouds began to roll in the air before us. I cowered far behind him in the protection of the brush nearby. No way was I going to face the blunt of this storm on the edge of that bluff. But there Harry stood, immovable. It must have taken nerves of steel.

*Graveyard Tour*

As I shook uncontrollably, Harry stood rock-solid. Both of his hands were outreached to the sky. His chanting grew louder and louder. He seemed larger than life, high up on that bluff, facing that storm. I expected lightning to cut right through him any minute."

"Then amid the dark and swirling clouds rolling in the sky, one cloud began to change. It was larger and brighter than the rest. It swirled and swayed and began throwing itself toward the ground. It spun and twisted its white funnel up and down in the sky. Harry called out at the top of his voice, *"And God will wipe away every tear from their eyes; there shall be no more death, nor sorrow, nor crying, and there shall be no more pain, for the former things have passed away."*

"As God as my witness," said Mr. Rich, "I saw what the Bible tells us. I saw the white horse! That enormous swirling cloud appeared before us like a giant white horse in the sky. My mind was shaken back to my youth, and I remembered Revelation 19: 11. I called aloud in the swirling rain and wind, *"Then I saw Heaven opened, and behold, a white horse. And He who sat upon him was called Faithful and True, and in Righteousness He judges and makes war."* All I could think was *King of Kings...Lord of Lords...save us all.* I was frightened beyond belief...and humbled. I stood paralyzed behind a large tree, trembling all over. I didn't want to watch. But as I peered from behind the safety of the tree, I could see Harry's silhouette against the flashing sky."

"Harry stood strong, both hands reaching to the sky. As he chanted many things, I heard these words on the air, rumbling in the sky. I heard them strong and clear. *"It is done, I am the Alpha and the Omega, the Beginning and the End. I will give of the fountain of the water of life freely to him who thirsts."*

"Harry raised his voice high, "Save my city...save those who know not the power of your destruction...your strength...your fairness. Save them, my Lord!"

"Then the words came. Those six devastating words came

through the chilling darkness. I cried aloud at their calling from the sky. It seemed as if the whole world was shouting at poor Harry. Winds shook his body. Rain pelted his skin. Wrath and fury ripped through the night sky. Those words rumbled in the fierce wind, and they shook me to the core. The very foundation of the mountain seemed to shake with their release. *"It doesn't work that way, Harry."*

"Thunder shook the mountain. Lightning seemed to flicker all about the night sky without ever touching the earth. Harry's fists trembled as he held them high. He fell to his knees, still calling to the sky, as it swirled and rumbled overhead. The pale cloud swirled and twisted its way around Harry, as the rain continued to pelt his ebony skin. And then, as quickly as it came, it dissipated, leaving Harry shaking uncontrollably on the mountainside. As the black clouds still rumbled and rolled, the pale cloud reentered the sky as intensely as it came. His prophesy had somehow been avoided. Livingston would not suffer that storm…but it came with a price. And, it was Harry who paid it."

"He lived about a year after that. I was a pallbearer at his funeral. There were only four of us. We couldn't find another two…two more that knew Harry for what he was. We couldn't find many that knew what Livingston had lost that winter, that winter of '33 when he died. We laid his body to rest after a long and painful year for him. He never really recovered after that fateful evening. Many folks said that he died of a broken heart. He had given all for his city…even warned it against its upcoming doom. When it would not listen, he took matters into his own hands…offering himself to balance the scales. *"It doesn't work that way, Harry."* Yet, Harry found a way.

"That's all I have to say, my friend."

The reporter sat speechless. His recorder clicked to a halt. He opened his mouth to speak, but nothing came out. Finally, he said, "Thank you very much, Mr. Rich. That was an amazing story. I don't know what to say."

*Graveyard Tour*

"You can say this, boy…you can tell me you will visit his grave. You can say that you will look at our beautiful courthouse with the same love as Harry. You can breathe the air in this valley between these high hills and love it. That would be a testimony to Harry. That would be something to be proud of."

\* \* \* \* \* \* \* \*

That young reporter was David Shuler. Although this interview with Mr. Rich was only one of several that he was working on, it somehow touched him, and he never viewed Livingston the same ever again. He looked closely at the buildings and walls near the court square and saw beautiful stonework. He paid closer attention to the world around him. He walked the grounds of Cash Cemetery and traced the inscribed letters of Harry's tombstone with his finger. He felt a connection somehow, and he wondered if anyone else had any knowledge about the stoneman that lie beneath the soil of this special little cemetery.

The interview for this project seemed more to him than just happenstance. Sure, it was a controversial topic, but it would no doubt gain him some notoriety in his line of work. He was still green around the collar from his recent graduation from Tennessee Tech in nearby Cookeville, but he was determined to make a career for himself. He felt that this particular story should just about make him an overnight success. That is, if he lived through his next interview.

# 3

### "Getting Happy"

David slept late. It's rare that he ever slept past 5:30 in the morning, but this day he did. He normally slapped a few pieces of bacon in a skillet and fried an egg or two, but not today. He just couldn't get the bones to move. Rather than making a greasy mess of the kitchen, he thought a nice brunch on the town would suit the situation. He could find grease and salt somewhere else this morning.

He stepped from the dull and colorless walls of his apartment, just off of the square. With one glance at his humble abode, it was obvious he was a young bachelor. He had no special keepsakes, no fancy family photos propped here and there. It was a simple flat of an aspiring young reporter. At least that's what he told himself. Some special lady would change all this eventually, but for now, it was…eclectic. Yeah…eclectic.

*Graveyard Tour*

One of his favorite haunts in Livingston was the Apple Dish. It was part restaurant and part antique mall. Half of the building was designated to the sale of clever little antiques from the past. It was called The Antique Market and possessed all the same charm as The Apple Dish. The other was set up as a wonderful little café venue along these pleasant streets of the city square. The entire county filled its booths during noontime, and the casual shoppers of antiques would often delay their day's shopping with a slice of pecan pie and a glass of fruit tea.

As he stepped through the door, he heard the familiar sound of the entry bell dangling above. The brass latch of the door had not functioned in decades so a simple pull on the door opened it. As he pulled, he listened for the dingle-dangle of its chime.

The desk clerk of the mall gave me her usual smile as she continued to talk briskly with a customer on the phone. She was Donna England…a pleasant and friendly gal with a warm smile and at least a paragraph of cheerful banter poised and ready for each customer walking through the door. She was a strong credit to her own business, and most of the locals knew her by name. David mouthed a silent "Hi, Donna" as he slipped into a booth next door. She continued her conversation on the phone as he looked for a waitress.

It wasn't long before Cindy walked up with her pen and tablet already unfolded. "Could I help you, Sir?"

Cindy was a playful sort, and she always insisted upon calling David *Sir*. There were only a few years difference in their age, yet she found it fun to joust a playful slam of age-related humor at him on a regular basis. "Many of our older folks like our special fruit tea. Might I bring you a glass?"

"Why yes," he replied, "could you ask Mommy if it's alright to do so?"

"I got your Mommy right here, smarty-pants…the usual?"

David just loved her playful flirting. Young or old, she could tease the best of them. She never failed to amuse him with her antics, and even though she was no swimsuit model, he found her attractive in every way. He could just sit and sip tea all day and toy with her. Her shoulder-length blond hair just knocked his socks off. He suspected she had the same effect on every other male in town.

"I'll take an order of grease and two sides of salt, please."

"It's too late for bacon and eggs, sleepy head, and I take offense to the "grease" comment. We only have "Proper" food here, Mr. Hangover. How about a club sandwich…you could pretend it's bacon and toast."

The gal knew him pretty well. His tongue was the size of a throw pillow, and his eyesight was still a little sparkly from the sports night party the night before. He and the boys often tipped a few cold ones during the game, and last night was no exception.

She smiled one of those rip-your-heart-out grins as she walked away without his order. She knew he'd eat whatever she brought… and love it. She could serve him garbage on a trash can lid and he would eat it with a smile. Huh, women.

He managed to tune out her bouncing blond hair long enough to refocus on his story. He had made arrangements with an old acquaintance for a visit late this morning. His acquaintance was old, but his age was that of David's. He had at one time been a close friend. But as time passed, David steered himself away from their friendship…mostly in fear.

Richard was a crude and tortured soul. He had always carried resentment for most of his family, and he never felt comfortable near them. As Richard grew older, he withdrew. He withdrew from family, from friends, from almost everyone he knew. And he did it for a reason.

Richard was deep in drugs. He was so deep that he never knew for certain where his next meal would come from. In fact, he just didn't care if he ate or not…lived or not. He was no more than one hundred forty pounds, and he was a big-boned fellow. His life was frightening to behold. And somehow, someway, he managed to find just the wrong people to call family. Those that provided support for him were the last ones he needed to do so. David did not want to see him today, but Richard had some valuable information.

David finished his *bacon and toast* and left Cindy a sizable tip. The smile alone was worth it. He offered Donna a wave on his way toward the door. When he noticed she was no longer on the phone, he knew right away his chances of leaving on time were unlikely.

"Hey, David, come here a minute."

"What have you got for me today, Donna?" he asked, still trying to leave in a timely manner.

"I saved back these old quill pens…thought they'd look good in your collection."

"I have half a dozen just like those," he replied with a playful grin.

"Oh…you know you *need* these. I can give you ten percent off."

"You know me pretty well, Donna. Oh, alright, keep them back, and I'll stop by tomorrow with some cash."

"I knew you'd want them. I'll just put them back here, and they will be ready whenever you want them."

"Thanks a bunch, Donna. I gotta run…I'll see you in a day or two." He gave Donna one last smile and waved on his way to the door. Donna was a good friend.

The bell above the door jingled as he skipped outside to the truck. He slid into the seat and turned the key. The engine fired up as David sat nervously at the wheel. "Might as well get this over with." He reluctantly pulled away from the Apple Dish and made a short drive across town.

Timidly, he gave a slight rap on the door of a row of apartment complexes he had always avoided. In his high school days, he knew never to go anywhere close to those buildings. They were a less than desirable location to visit, and those that did, never lingered long enough than to make a *delivery*, then creep away. He felt he could make a quick visit during the bright daylight hours, but no way would he have lurked here in darkness. There was enough darkness in this subdivision, even in daylight.

A shaky and paranoid Richard answered the door. He quickly scanned the streets behind David and motioned him in. Without so much as a *Hello*, he jabbed a question at David. "You bring it?"

"Yeah, man," he replied, with a hint of distaste. "I got it. Good to see you, too."

He stood shaking before David with his eyes nervously dancing around in his head. David's heart broke for him, yet he could tell that he was no longer the playful friend of his youth. His years had weathered him beyond any semblance of his earlier days. David was not at all comfortable.

David then noticed another fellow in the shadows. He nervously stared the fellow down and showed no signs of fear, even though his heart pounded a mile a minute. The fellow eventually walked up to Richard and handed him a package. He then turned to David and held out his hand in request.

David looked at Richard with a questioning glance.

He nodded his head in reply, and David did not hesitate. He extended a one hundred dollar bill toward the man, and he yanked it from his grasp. Within a split second, the man was out the door and gone. It was now David's turn to look around suspiciously. He could just see his name in his own newspaper for drug conspiracy. *That would look great on my resume'.*

"Is this how you live?" David asked.

"If you call it living," he responded. "You have no idea what it's like. I friggin' got no life." His hands shook uncontrollably as he fidgeted with numerous items of paraphernalia David had never seen. There were grotesque and filthy needles about the room that he began to gather up. He made several feeble attempts to *wipe* them clean on his shirt. He went through a nasty series of unbelievable procedures to prepare his dope. David tried to make small talk while watching the horrid ritual going on before him. "We'll...uhh...we'll talk in a minute," he said, completely oblivious to David's presence. He could not have cared less whether David was there watching this ugly display or not.

He struggled to twist an old t-shirt into a knot around his arm. He hyper-ventilated continuously, as he worked. Just when things could get no uglier, he turned pale green in color. Seconds later, he vomited uncontrollably all over the floor, still nervously shaking head to toe. He struggled to focus in the near darkness. He finally regained himself and began twisting the T-shirt around his arm again. David fought back every urge to vomit also, as he watched that needle enter Richard's vein. He had thumped every vein in his arm, just trying to find one soft enough to inject. It was one disgusting display of human filth.

As the contents of the needle entered Richard's vein, he released the tension on the T-shirt. His eyes rolled and his weight shifted back into the chair. One could almost see the burn of the heroin creeping up his arm. As his head bobbled side to side, he looked to David with glassy eyes. "We...we...can talk now, brother," he mumbled.

By now, David could barely remember what he had come to talk about. He was sick to his stomach and completely frightened that the police would storm the place any minute. He wished he was not there. He could have remembered Richard for what he once was. He could have reflected on fond memories from their youth. But, that was now out of the question. This gut-wrenching phenomenon had shaken him to the core, and he would now remember Richard this way forever.

David finally decided that since he had gone this far and had viewed what he had, that he might as well talk about why he came. He had a few odd questions for Richard and expected that he (even in his condition) could probably still answer with little trouble. David broke the awkward silence. "You want to tell me a little about witchcraft?"

Back in high school, the two had had a number of long conversations about this subject. Back then, David was thirsty to learn about all types of religion, and Richard shared with him a new and highly-misunderstood version of witchcraft that based most of their beliefs on some of the old nature-worshipping pagans of long ago. He would always say, "We try not to call it witchcraft…gets people all scared and defensive. It's not about evil. It's just a natural and spiritual religion, designed to do good."

Richard had read and studied numerous books on the subject, and David knew that of all people around here, it would be Richard that could give a straight-up answer. That was the trouble with Richard, though. He *could* give a straight answer, but always chose to keep things vague enough that it would make one study for one's self.

"Witchcraft," he began, "is a lot like guns." His eyes were still glassy, but he was speaking plainly. "All religion…is a lot like guns. Guns can save you from the bowels of death. They can also rape and pillage and cause great death and destruction. They can be a beginning…and an end. So can religion. The long and razor-sharp blade of religion is sharp on both edges, my friend. One must know how to wield it…or face the bloody consequences."

*Graveyard Tour*

Richard had always had a way with words. It was a shame that such a talent for storytelling had been wasted by a life of drugs. His words had always been poignant. He could have been great. Instead, he sat in the hazy gloom of this disgusting apartment, just lingering in this world.

"But you didn't come here to listen to my thoughts on religion, now did ya?" He paused and gave a feeble chuckle as he wiped away a few drops of blood from his arm. "You came here to hear about the creepy stuff. I gotta tell ya, man, when you're high on drugs…that creepy junk is a blast. It's exhilarating! It'll raise the hair on the back of your neck…get ya all tingly inside. Hell, it's a hey-day. It gets ya all fired up and crazy." He paused and gritted his teeth with disgust. "And then one day you wake up in some cemetery with the blood of some poor animal smeared all over ya, and your head's pounding like God's in there making amends. And then it creeps in on ya…just sorta creeps in through the back door of your brain and eats at it." He paused and stared into the distance, like there was something haunting his memory. His eyes squinted closed, and a look of anguish came over his face. "Here," he said, finally pulling himself back into the present and handing David a couple of paperback books. "Everything you *don't* want to know is in here. One's the good book…the other's the naughty book. Don't say I didn't warn you."

David took the books from his hand and reached to his other for a handshake. David's hand engulfed Richard's boney palm, and he grasped it tightly. The two looked long and hard into one another's eyes without saying a word. When Richard finally broke the silence, his words ripped through David's stomach like a chainsaw. "Don't go tippin' the scales, David. It don't work that way."

David's jaw nearly hit the floor. He had heard that phrase just a little too often these last two days. He let go of Richard's hand and walked to the door. As he turned the knob to leave, he glanced back over his shoulder at Richard. He was already thumping his arm for another injection. David shook his head and pulled the door closed behind him.

*Darren Shell*

It was a great relief to leave that porthole to Hell. David's lungs took in as much fresh air as they could hold. It eased the discomfort in his stomach, and he raised his face to the sunshine, feeling its rays as a rejuvenating shower of warmth. He couldn't help but think that if every high-school kid could have witnessed what he just had, then maybe there would be much less substance abuse these days. It might just scare them down the straight road. He was more than elated to leave, and a straight road away from here was his first objective.

It was time to take his thoughts away from the ugliness he had witnessed this morning. One does not have to go far in Livingston to raise one's spirits, especially on a sunny February day. Most days of February were not this pleasant, and he was inspired to take a refreshing walk through town.

He parked his old pickup on the square and hit the streets on foot. He paused for several minutes before leaving the square, just taking in the courthouse. He had always marveled at the architecture of the old building here on the square. It was a simple and square structure, yet possessed a quaint hometown charm. Its colorful bricks shone warmly in the late morning sun, and the reflections in the glass of the windows added a rich and historic feel to the old building. He tried to imagine how it must have looked after the Civil War when it was burned down to a vacant shell. It seemed fruitless that *any* side from this war would burn the courthouse. What good could that have done? The town just had to build it back with what little funding was available at the time. But war rarely makes sense, especially back then when neighbors fought neighbors, and friends fought friends. There was nothing *civil* about that war. *But that's enough war*, he thought to himself. *I'm trying to get happy.*

He elected to walk down Church Street to the old railroad station. The railroad had long since shut down, and even the buildings nearby were crumbling in decay. What few businesses still surviving in this old part of town almost seemed to cling to yesteryear…existing where buildings and rent were still inexpensive. It was a nice little trip back in time for him, but he was used to seeing this part of town.

*Graveyard Tour*

The old newspaper still operated in the old downtown building of its youth, and he worked there five days a week. Mr. Mitchell usually gave him Tuesdays off. Since the paper came out on Wednesday, normally the printing process was happening on Tuesday, and he could save David's labor for Wednesday's many deliveries. David didn't bother stopping in. He could almost feel the last-minute rushes of publishing from outside the building.

He elected to walk the streets behind *The Enterprise* on the south-eastern edges of old town. Although he had often traveled these streets by truck, his leisurely walk today lightened his mood. He meandered through the many side streets and driveways of this section of housing, remarking to himself about the comfortable feel of the place. The houses here were neither lavish, nor run-down, neither filthy nor spotless. In fact, they appeared to be in no extreme whatsoever. They felt homey and pleasant. Bicycles were evident in most yards and the occasional basketball lay abandoned in a driveway or two. It seemed as neighborly as any community he had ever walked.

And another interesting part of this section of town was its cemeteries. It seemed that nearly every street had its own tiny cemetery. Most were very old and small and desolate, yet well-maintained and beautiful in their own right. He was surprised by the number of them here. David had always been drawn to old cemeteries, and these were as intriguing as any he had seen before, especially given that they were right here in the subdivisions where the kids played ball, and hide-and-seek, and the like. They seemed a perfectly natural part of the landscape, and no one had any qualms about it at all.

He made a turn and walked back toward Main Street. As he reached the old library building, he made a left and walked slowly back toward the square. This little jaunt by the old library was one of his favorites. He paused and ran his hand along the rock wall at his side. It had been there for years, and David knew why. This was a Harry Springs wall, and it showed all of its original strength. Only now, this old Livingston Landmark was warm with time-worn patina and years of loving hands brushing against its old stone. Its tiny crevices still contained much of its old mortar and traces of bright green moss, clinging to its surface. The old wall had energy. It had that *Harry Springs* feel. David smiled and continued on his way.

By now, his wanderings through downtown Livingston were beginning to make him hungry. This "getting happy" can take a lot out of a fellow. And strangely, he really was happy. Between the sunshine and the quaint streets of town, he had shaken the uglies from his head and felt better about the whole thing. And since he was hungry and getting happy, why not take another venture over to the Apple Dish? That little blond could help him with both.

**"File Thirteen"**

It's uncertain why David chose that topic for his first report. In hindsight, he wished he had not chosen such a touchy story altogether. He could have studied some special building or cemetery to write about in his first real story for *The Enterprise*. It might have at least gotten published. He could remember the look on Mr. Mitchell's face when he dropped it on his desk.

"What the Hell is this? What are you…nuts? This is Livingston, Tennessee. You'll have hate mail on day one. I think you can stick to selling ads and taking photos for awhile. Make the locals love you before you make them hate you."

David looked him in the eye, wondering how he could be so judgmental. He hadn't even read it yet, and he was quickly tossing it aside. Yet, looking back, David suspected that Mr. Mitchell may have had a point. This was one tight little community, and sometimes the tiniest of waves could become tidal.

He picked up his report from Mr. Mitchell's desk. He was really disappointed. He had worked hard on that project. He had risked his life in places he did not want to be caught dead in. So, that bundle of nicely-typed paper sat quietly on his desk until he could make the locals love him…whatever that meant.

And, David eventually forgot that old report. It was really far too long-winded for the paper anyway. It would have taken a number of weeks to get the whole story out, and it probably would have gotten pulled anyway. He still took it off the pile on his desk now and then to dust its cover and reminisce. "*Modern Witchcraft in the Upper Cumberland*…people would have ate it up." It was creepy, yet informative. And in all honesty, most would have found it intriguing and interesting to read. But it eventually found its way to his file cabinet at home and lived there with Richard's two books…biding time.

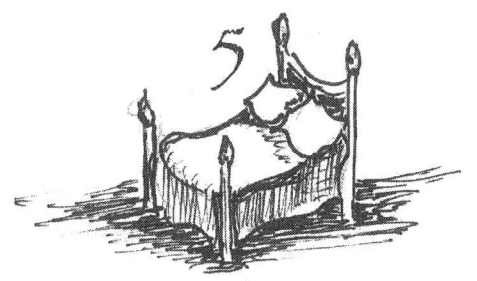

**"An Interview with Ms. Copeland"**

$S$eptember, 1985

"Why yes, Lord yes…my Great Granny used to tell it all the time. If we wouldn't get our chores done on time…or clean up dinner just so…she'd say *I'll send Granny Mary to come get ya.* Lord, child, that's all it'd take. We'd scamper like peas a fallin' from a pod. We were all scared to death that Granny Mary was coming to get us. When we got older, we found out what really happened.

Now, let me see. I wanna tell it like Granny woulda. It was the 1830s. Weren't much law around here then, but then again, it don't take much law to know what happens when two women get ta feudin', and one gets murdered. My Granny Mary (I don't know how many 'Greats' she was) killed Ruth Daugherty! Stabbed her with one of them ol' hog-butcherin' knives. Poor Ruth must not have known what hit her. I guess that there were signs posted all over the place.

## WANTED FOR THE MURDER OF RUTH DAUGHERTY: MARY COPELAND, WIFE OF LITTLE JOE COPELAND, LOCAL BUSINESSMAN

Now, nobody knew for sure what really happened. Some say Little Joe had been a messin' with Ruth on the side, and Mary put a stop to it. I guess nobody knows for sure, but Granny Mary sure killed her dead…killed her plum dead.

She ran off some place and hid for a long time. I guess she finally came back when things cooled down a bit…you know… sorta let everybody's temper chill a little. She faced her charges in the Supreme Court and won on the grounds of self-defense. She and Little Joe lived here the rest of their life…pert-near forty more years. I think it always bothered her, though. I remember how Granny described the night Mary died. It scares me somethin' terrible to think about it. Sure glad it wasn't me in that bed. Chills me to the bone!

Granny Mary was on her death bed…been sick some time, I guess. They lived in a house on the hill above where the golf course is now. They lived someplace up in the hollow there in Hidden Valley. Little Joe was with her when she was dyin', and some fella was tryin' to doctor her up.

Granny said she was watchin' real close to Mary, lying in that bed. Little Joe and the doctor fella was prayin' and tryin' to calm her down. Said she was almost crazy in the bed…all tremblin' and shakin' and starin' at the foot of the bed. She kept cryin' out loud, "She's come for me…get her away from me!" Granny said that even in her feeble condition, Mary sat straight up in the bed and slid

*Graveyard Tour*

back against the wall screaming "No!" Both of her hands were held out in front of her like she was defendin' herself from somebody. All of a sudden, her eyes got real big and her mouth fell open. Both of her hands grabbed her chest, and she slid down in the bed…stone dead…almost like she was stabbed. Little Joe had to know Ruth had come for her. Just puts the fear of God in ya…thinkin' maybe Ruth had come back for her, after all those years.

Joe fixed her up a right-nice grave on the hill where they lived. He fixed 'em both one, just alike. Had her name carved all nice on hers and even on his own. He was gettin' up in years too and figgered he might as well get 'em both made up. They was nice graves, too, with those big flat slabs of slate rock. Joe had a good bit of money, for around these parts, and he could afford them nice graves. He was the one that rebuilt the courthouse, you know…after they burned it during the Civil War. He made a good bit of money there.

Funny thing happened though. He visited that grave bunches when he could, but he didn't live all that long after her. But this is the strange thing…her grave ain't got no marks on it…none. It's like them words just up and disappeared. Granny said she seen 'em with her own eyes…and then, later on, they were gone. Gone!

Town folk said Ruth took 'em…took the letters plum off the rocks! Said she wanted to be buried with Little Joe…not some murderer there beside him. That's plum scary, I say…plum scary. I don't go up there no more. Them graves can just grow up with briars for all I care."

\* \* \* \* \*

"Are they still there, Ms. Copeland?" asked David, scratching down a crude map on his notepad.

"Why sure…but I ain't a going. They're up there on that high road above the golf course. You can't miss 'em. They're right next to the road, just over the hill."

*Darren Shell*

"I think that's all I need, Ms. Copeland," said David, as he gathered his notes to leave. "I thank you for your time. The story should be in the paper in a few weeks. We have a little history column where we write up these types of stories, and yours should be coming up soon. I'll see to it that you get a copy."

"You just come right back now, if you have any questions."

"Thanks again," he said as he stepped out the door. "I'll let you know when it comes out."

David's truck wound its way back down the crooked road from Alpine to Livingston. He fought the urge to pull into the Apple Dish for a quick bite. He really needed to be getting some typing done back at the office, and he knew he wouldn't want to leave once he got in the door. He had managed to talk Cindy into a number of dates lately, and they both seemed to be hitting it off quite well, despite the fact that on nearly every date he had stopped what they were doing long enough to investigate some breaking story. *This won't take but a minute, dear.* Yeah, right.

He finished out his day at work by completing his assignment about Mary Copeland. By now he had learned what Mr. Mitchell wanted from his work, and Mr. Mitchell had become accustomed to letting David handle all the odd and bizarre stories. He could really capture a mood in his writing, and no one else really wanted the doom and gloom stories anyway. He had found his niche at the *Enterprise*. So, between the creepy historical stories from the past, and the weekly bloody car crashes, David found himself quite busy on the old typewriter. And that suited him just fine. Each week was an exciting new story.

**"An Interview with Mr. McDonald"**

**"C**ome in, Mr. Shuler, and have a seat."

"Thank you, Sir," said David, as he placed his recorder on the desk in front of him.

"I record nothing, Mr. Shuler," he said, with a dry and unwelcoming tone.

"Sorry, Sir, I just have a terrible memory, and it keeps my facts straight for me. We really don't need it today…I don't intend to take much of your time."

*Darren Shell*

"I, too, am sorry for the burden, but we lawyers are not a trusting sort."

"No problem at all, Mr. McDonald. I'll try to keep this short and to-the-point."

"Oh, not at all, Mr. Shuler, I have an hour scheduled for you."

"Please…call me David. I will make this quick. I know you are a busy man."

"Yes, yes…that is an unfortunate side effect of my business… but let us speak of what you came to hear. I don't often counsel off-the-clock. Carry on."

David quickly looked at his watch. Ten past two. Better hurry.

"Could you give me some insight on the murder of Mr. Cy McDonald…Marshall of Overton County just after the Civil War?"

"Now, that's a long way back, my friend. I'll tell you what I know, for what its worth. My grandfather, who was also an attorney here in town, told me the story years ago. I am not much of a historian, but I know some of what happened."

"The Civil War was ending…I say ending…even when it ended, it seemed to drag on for years. My great-grandfather watched his father (I guess my double-great-grandfather) stomp from the family kitchen. He and his wife had been arguing miserably for almost an hour, as he reached for the doorknob to leave. Before he stepped outside, he shouted a string of sentences at her. "Somebody's got to do something. They've burned the courthouse. People are robbing households left and right…and now…NOW…they've built a moonshine still big enough to float the dad-gummed ark in whiskey! Who else is gonna do it, honey? Somebody's got to end it!" He slammed the door of the house and marched out to his horse. And as the sound of galloping hooves filled the yard, his words seemed to hang in the air of their kitchen. Those were the last words his family ever heard him speak."

"What happened?"

"Well, I don't suppose anyone has an accurate assessment of what truly happened, but this is the gist of it. It seems that Grandpa Cy found the still. It was supposedly not all that far out of town, just a mile or two north. There was a large spring and cave in the area, and I guess that is where the still had been set up. They say it was an exceptionally large still. I don't suppose the likes of which has ever been built in these parts. It reportedly produced hundreds and hundreds of gallons of whiskey. As I have been told, the finished product was kept in the confines of the cave, which was nearly impossible to find if you did not know its precise location. There was something about its entrance that camouflaged it in some way… water, trees, whatever. Anyway, it must have been a perfect locale for the project. But, it was too big an operation for some back woods boys to handle. It had to be funded locally, somehow…it was an enormous operation, and somebody with clout had to have been at the helm. Anyway, Cy didn't come home. Rumors spread, and it was said that he had been buried in the shine cave so nobody would ever find him…and so nobody would ever come looking for him."

"And time passed…a bunch of it. Seventy years ticked away, as Cy's family waited and wondered what ever happened to him. And then one day…out of the blue…a bag of **bones** showed up on my grandfather's desk, here in town. Yeah, **bones**. After some investigation, it was determined that they were my great-great-grandfather's, retrieved from a cave north of town. Go figure. I am forced to think that someone involved in the killing must have died…and those in-the-know wished to make amends. Why else would anyone even remember a seventy-year-old murder? It just doesn't make sense. I am certain that it was a means to an end for somebody. *Somebody* wanted it off their conscience."

David rummaged through his pants pocket and retrieved a piece of folded paper. "I have the article from the paper from the thirties…

if you want it."

"Oh, I have it. Look on the wall behind you. It is framed nicely for me to view every day of my life. I hope that somehow…some way…that something good may come of it, yet, although that seems unlikely now. I suppose it will always be a snippet from the old days…destined to obscurity. It's history, I guess. "

David sneaked a look at his watch. Three o'clock. Better be moving on. "I suppose I should be on my way. Thanks so much, Mr. McDonald. You have been very kind. It's a sad story for your family, but I appreciate you telling me…thanks a bunch. The story should be in the history column, soon. I'll make sure you get a copy."

"Oh, I appreciate a good story, Mr. Shuler…ya never know what could stem from history!"

"Yes, Sir, thanks again."

\* \* \* \* \*

By now, it was late afternoon, and David was starving. And quite frankly, that meant two things wrapped into one…Apple Dish. David was constantly starving for two things…food and Cindy. She had not only become accustomed to David's visits, but expected them quite often. The two had become nearly inseparable, and she was always happy to see him popping through the door, beaming with energy. She constantly joked with him, "You know, the sooner you marry me…the skinnier you'll be. Another month of cheeseburgers, and I might just turn you down. It is *ME* you love, right?"

And love her he did. Although his over-the-top work ethic often offended her, she knew…in her heart…that he truly loved her. And that's a big deal. He always let her know how much he loved her, and he let her know that she was special. The ugly head of work would sometimes show itself, but David tried to keep it at bay. The life of a reporter is sometimes choppy…here a minute, there

*Graveyard Tour*

another. But Cindy knew that up front…and she had fallen head-first in love with him.

"Let's see," he said, "I'll take a…"

"Shut up, already. I saw you coming." She smiled her playful smile and placed a plate of the daily special in front of him. He replied with his usual quiet laugh and took her hand.

"It really is you."

"Me what?"

"You…that I love."

"Awhhhhhh," moaned the crowd around them. By now, the crowd of the Apple Dish had come to love their pair of lovebirds. Young and old now knew them and looked forward to their playful comments here in the café…which were nearly everyday. They were a common fixture here, and the love in their hearts was contagious to all around.

"Yeah…one of those. That's just what I wanted. How ever could you have known?"

"Just eat it and be quiet, Mr. Reporter Man. We ladies-in-waiting tire of you brutes ordering this and that. Always the waitress…never the bride. Ho-hum."

"Ummmmmm," sayeth the crowd.

David chuckled and ate his food as Cindy bounced to the back room to work. He glanced over at Mrs. Easterly, who was raising her eyebrows and giving him her best *shame-on-you* look.

He returned a reassuring wink at her, as he emptied the contents of his pocket on the tip tray. He left the table and walked to the door, pausing to watch his table.

Cindy bounced back to the table, disappointed in missing David's departure. She sensed something strange…David never left without saying good bye. As she lifted the ten dollar bill David had left on the tray, she found a lovely diamond engagement ring beneath. She raised her tear-filled eyes to the door. There stood David…smiling ear-to-ear.

"YES!" she shouted, as she slid the ring on her finger. "YES!"

The Apple Dish roared with enthusiasm.

**"New Beginnings"**

March 9, 1986

David and Cindy were wed on a perfect Saturday in February. The wedding was held just out of town in the back yard of a family friend. The weather was as lovely as any February day could be. A few friends and family were present, and David was given strict orders…YOU WILL COVER NO STORIES UNTIL LONG AFTER THE HONEYMOON!

David always claimed that the honeymoon was worthy of many stories, but that needs no comment.

A few weeks later, the reception was hosted at The Apple Dish, and many, many family members and friends attended. It was a

*Darren Shell*

great party, and most of Livingston was there to celebrate. There was food galore, and old man Ledbetter ate over thirty of his favorite pig-in-a-blanket sausages. "Best friggin' reception I ever been to!" Some folks pondered how many receptions he had ever really been invited to, but that probably needs no comment, either.

"It is now time for the bride and groom to take part in the first dance. Could you both come forward?"

"David…..David?"

Cindy stood quietly on the dance floor with a solemn look on her face. "Hel-*lo!*"

"Yeah, honey…just a minute." David nervously talked away to a friend. "You're kidding? No way!" David was taking quick notes on a scratch pad and listening closely to the man's words.

"David….David?"

"Just a minute, honey."

"David?"

"Honey…I gotta go…I'll be right back…dance with your father. Really…I'll be right back…it's the biggest drug bust in the county's history…I can't miss it! Really…I'll be right back." He jumped out the door to his truck and disappeared from the parking lot.

"Fine, David…" said Cindy, quietly. "I'm not the biggest anything…"

\* \* \* \* \*

The next four years of David and Cindy's life changed little. The rush of everyday life seemed to engulf them both. They had not taken a vacation since their honeymoon, and both were overdue for some time off.

But, that time off just didn't seem to happen until the fall of 1990. Cindy gave birth to a seven pound baby girl. Molly Katheryn Shuler was born into this world with the most beautiful blue eyes and a trace of the same wavy blond hair as her mother. She was strong and healthy and was without question the single greatest component in their lives. She would grow to possess the same fiery spirit of her mother, and the same nose-to-the-grindstone work ethic of her father. She would be successful in life, no doubt. And despite the nonstop grind of David's job, he did make some time for the two girls of his life…just not quite as much as they wished.

\* \* \* \* \*

The next decade unfolded for the Shulers, much like the years prior, with one exception. Cindy backed away from work to raise Molly, while David sank farther into his job to keep the ends meeting. And as Molly grew into a beautiful young lady, David mostly missed it.

# 8

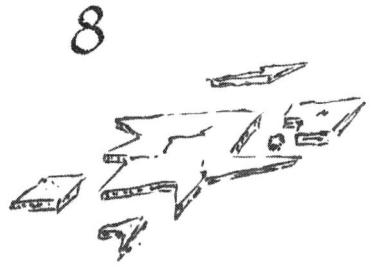

**"Rush"**

D̲ecember 2000

"We're gonna be late you know?" growled Cindy, checking her watch.

"I'm sorry," said David, "I don't know what you want me to do about it. I'm already driving faster than I'd rather. She won't have to wait long."

"It's cold. I don't want her standing outside in the dark waiting for us."

*Graveyard Tour*

"She won't be outside. I'm sure one of the other parents will stick around for an extra five minutes. Practice might not even be over. There will be someone at the church for a few extra minutes anyway. I hope she still has on her practice costume. She's the prettiest elf in the whole play."

"Let's just get there before she freezes over, okay?"

"I'm not going any faster. There are hundreds of deer in this hollow. Just last week…"

David stopped mid-sentence as a flash of color darted from the ditch line. In less than a second, a pair of antlers crashed through the windshield of the car, eliminating David's view of the road entirely. He had already applied the brakes and was swerving away from the oncoming danger. But it was too late. There was no stopping the brute force of the deer's carcass crashing into the front seat of the car.

The car left the road and plowed through a small fencerow, before ramming into an embankment. What was left of the deer's body ejected itself back out of the car and into the field, revealing the massive injuries sustained by Cindy.

David raised his bloody and broken nose from the steering wheel just long enough to view the carnage. Blood filled his eyes as he tried to focus. His head pounded with pain, as he tried to gather his senses. He simply could not focus in his shaken world. One of the car's headlights survived the crash and shown nearly straight upward. The cold night air burned his nostrils as he choked and gagged. Then, in many ways, David Shuler's world went black.

\* \* \* \* \* \*

David awakened in the hospital two days later with Molly waiting by his bed. David's mother and father were there, as well as Cindy's parents. David had miraculously survived the crash. Cindy…had not. She died in the car only minutes after David caught his last glimpse of her in the darkness of the wreck. That particular vision was the only thing he ever remembered about the accident, and it haunted his memory with guilt and anguish.

They laid Cindy to rest on the outskirts of Livingston, and Molly and David began trying to pick up enough pieces of their lives to make the puzzle still fit together without Cindy. And quite frankly…there were few pieces left to place.

Young girls need a mother more than a father…yet; the father is the next best thing. Only Molly didn't really have that. David submersed himself even more into his work. He fruitlessly used his job as a distraction from the pain and guilt in his heart. Although the accident was not really David's fault, he just could not forgive himself for not having missed the inevitable collision with the deer. He felt he had taken Molly's mother away from her, and he felt that awful pang in his heart every time he looked into her eyes. David's parents picked up on his dilemma right away and immediately began keeping Molly as much as possible to ease his load. Before long, most of Molly's time was spent with the grandparents. They nurtured her and loved her and tended her every need with great compassion. But that does not replace a mother. And although Molly grew into a beautiful and intelligent young woman, she missed her mother dearly…and missed her father just a little more each day.

# 9

**"It All Started So Simple"**

Tuesday, October 10, 2006

The lunch room of Livingston Academy High School was busy with the hustle and bustle of teenagers filing in and out. A constant rotation of students emptied from the classrooms and into the commons area for their lunchtime meal. The puke-inducing scent of green bean casserole filled the air, as Molly Shuler slapped her plate down next to her group of friends.

"This stuff gags me," she commented, as she wrinkled her sixteen year old nose.

"Oh, shut up and eat the macaroni and cheese like everybody

else," said one of her best friends. He was Allen, a local descendant of the founding fathers of Livingston. His family owned hundreds of acres of land around the area and lived in a lavish home just outside of town. The fencing in their pastures alone was more valuable than most of the subdivisions in town. But that was the beauty of their family. Despite their outside appearances of extreme wealth, they donated money to the betterment of their city almost dollar-for-dollar of their net worth. For every dollar of fencing they owned, someplace in Livingston there was an equally impressive city structure lovingly donated by them. Many locals held a jealousy in their hearts toward them, but anyone that truly knew them understood without question that they had earned every one of their numerous dollars and were generous enough to share their wealth. And despite coming from a family of "money", and being quite an attractive and popular young lad, Allen still managed to be a kind-hearted fellow, well-respected amid friends and townspeople.

"I can't think of anything this so-called *food* could be useful for," said Molly, distastefully.

It only took a split second for Scotty to speak up. "I bet it could hold a turd together." Scotty was the self-proclaimed "resident smart-aleck". Every crowd has one. Nobody ever really invited him. He just always seemed to be near…kind of like how your favorite T-shirts just seem to be near the top of the pile in the dresser drawer. It's unlikely that Scotty was anyone's favorite, but he just seemed to gravitate to the top of the pile.

"You're disgusting," she said with another wrinkle of her nose.

"I'm sorry," he said with grin, "I didn't mean to turn ya on."

"Oh Scotty, you couldn't turn on a *security light*." She plopped down in her seat and tried not to notice him.

Molly's good friend Katie raised her voice. "Did you bring it? You got me all excited!"

*Graveyard Tour*

"Yeah," she said, "I tried to look it over last night, but there is a lot of weird stuff in here. This first book is all about happy stuff... you know...love potions, boyfriend spells, all kinds of teenage yuppie stuff."

"What else ya got?" asked Allen.

"Well," she commented, "Dad's report is kinda vague. It's got lots of neat references to stuff in these books, but I don't think you'd care much for it. But this last book...this one here...that's some funky crap."

"I just love that fowl mouth of yours, Molly," said Scotty, giggling to himself. "What else can you do with it?"

"I can tell Ms. Stevens who put the condoms in her purse for everyone to see."

"Sorry, dear...just joking..."

"Could you two shut up long enough for us to make a plan?" Allen was the ring-leader of this group, and all involved listened to his words as if they were gospel.

"So when we goin'?" asked Molly. "I'm afraid the law will be out all over the place on Halloween. You know everybody is gonna be watchin' everything, every place."

"That's why we're going Friday."

"Why Friday?" asked Scotty, as if he was intended to be a part of the conversation.

"It's Friday the thirteenth. Why would we need Halloween when we got Friday the thirteenth?" asked Allen, with a mischievous grin. "We'll have all the fun while everybody else waits for the law to find them on Halloween."

"Good idea!" exclaimed Scotty. "We'll *GITTER DONE* before anybody knows we've even been there."

"Who invited you, Scotty?" asked Allen.

"You know I ain't gonna miss it! You done let me hear about it! Hell, I'm ready to go right now!"

"You in, Katie?" asked Molly.

"Yeah, I guess. Can I bring Callie? She's supposed to be spending the night with me on Friday. I don't have any choice, there. Momma promised my Aunt Sherry she could stay with us. She won't be a problem. We've let her hang with us before."

"I'll baby-sit," chided Scotty, with an obvious air of excitement. He could remember Callie's last trip here where he managed to act as chaperone. She had secretly downed two beers from the family fridge and "floated" around all evening, needing personal guidance. He felt compelled to offer his assistance, being the kind soul he was.

"Why is she always staying with you?" asked Allen.

"It's her momma. She's bad sick. She needs an operation on her back…some sort of spine thing. They don't have the money. They've had a benefit or two, but it isn't anywhere enough to cover the surgery. I just feel sorry for Callie. She needs to get her mind off of it. My mom has her stay with us…and I don't really mind. She is a sweetheart."

"So we're all in. All agreed?" asked Allen. His question was more of a command, as he looked into three other sets of eyes. "We got me and Molly, Katie and Callie, and of course…*Scotty*."

"Done deal?" he asked, looking at their nodding heads. "Then it's settled. Friday night…we'll meet at Dairy Queen, say 8 o'clock. Then it's Old Union…Church and Cemetery."

"Got your books, Molly?"

"Yep."

"Good, let me have them. I need to study a little. I got everything else. Bring your flashlights…and your nerve. This could be a night to remember!"

**"Bad Ideas"**

Friday, October 13, 8:00 p.m.

The lights from Dairy Queen seemed to illuminate the entire parking lot, as this group parked and prepared for their trip. They had all the essentials…witchcraft books, Ouija board, crow bar, a series of strange and aromatic herbs and roots, dried and prepared for this special occasion. Here they all sat, nervous and exhilarated, almost panting with anticipation. Five young people timidly occupied space in the Dairy Queen parking lot anxiously looking forward to their simple little prank of fun that was about to unfold, and they were all itching with excitement.

*Graveyard Tour*

"I can't imagine anything uglier than calling up the dead," said Molly.

"How about a sack of assholes?" asked Scotty, grinning like the doughnut guy near the Jenny Craig clinic.

"How about I polish my toenails on your intestines?" asked Molly.

"Oh, not right now, honey, but maybe we could play later." Scotty had no morals whatsoever.

"Get in the car and shut up." Molly was losing patience. She normally would have had at least one come-back to slam him with, but her mind was far from here tonight. There was much more to think about than their petty bantering.

"This stuff ain't real, is it Allen?" she asked.

"Oh, I doubt it. It's just spooks and spells somebody wrote down to sell paperbacks. Look at the cover. If that wouldn't sell books, what would?" Allen had a point. The cover was fantastic, even with its age. It had symbols and crosses and candles, all hovering over a dark and eerie graveyard. You may not judge a book by its cover, but you can sure sell one with it. This book could have been popular by its cover alone.

"It just worries me. Yeah, I'm excited. It's all creepy and dark...but I just don't feel right about it."

"Don't go all scaredy-cat on me, now. We're all in, right?"

All nodded in agreement, and Molly finally succumbed to their pressure. "Yeah, I guess."

It was a perfect night to be out. It was sixty-five degrees and a faint breeze cooled the air. Every star in the night sky was visible, as Allen turned the key to his crew cab pickup. The loud rumble of the diesel under the hood seemed to only add to the energy of the group. *Are you ready to rumble?!!!!!*

Allen's truck seemed to know the way to Old Union on its own. Allen talked the entire trip, discussing several details of their plan and reciting certain phrases from the books. In a matter of fifteen minutes, the pickup turned off of Highway 85 and onto Old Union Road.

"Why Old Union?" asked Molly, with a pang of discomfort in her stomach.

"Because it's the most haunted place in Overton County, that's why." Allen continued to talk as he drove. "Remember last year when Donnie and Mick and the boys came out here? They were looking for the lights everybody talks about…you know…the old folks talking about music and lights coming from inside the building. The locks are on the *outside* of the doors. There couldn't be anybody in there. The boys said they saw it…big as life. They said the doors rattled and light shown all around the jam of the door…but not the windows. Those were pitch dark."

Everybody sat speechless in their seats as Allen told his tale. "I thought this place would be ideal. That's what the crowbar is for. One swift tug with this and that old hasp should fall to the ground. Then, we're in!"

"Then what?" asked Scotty, who had been too preoccupied with Callie's presence to keep up with the conversation.

"Then we follow the instructions in the book and call out the names we've chosen. If you haven't decided on a name yet, I'd suggest you pull one from Molly's dad's file. Call on someone if you have a question you want to ask about Livingston…or something that happened a long time ago, whatever. There are bunches of neat characters in that folder of reports."

"Allen, did you pick a name?"

"You bet! I'm calling Mr. Harry Springs."

"Why him?"

"I wanna know if he saw the white horse over Livingston…like it says in the article. That had to be far-out! I wanna know what he saw."

"Neat choice," said Katie. "I'm gonna call Cy McDonald. I wanna know where that cave is."

"What cave?" asked Scotty.

"The moonshine cave, where they buried him…don't you read?"

Scotty and Callie were in the back seat leafing through the old manuscripts. "This one looks cool. Little Joe Copeland…Dad always said that guy left some treasure in the courthouse when he built it. I forgot about him until I read his name here. I think his wife murdered some gal in town, too. I think I'll call on him."

"I never heard about treasure in the courthouse," said Allen.

"Don't you read?" Scotty chided. "Actually, they say he left clues or something inside. I don't know. Dad's been all over the place inside there and ain't found nothin'. I don't really care who his wife killed…I just want his treasure."

Callie spoke up. "Then I'll call his wife!"

"Excellent!" chimed Allen.

"How about you, Molly?"

"I haven't decided yet," she said dejectedly, as she let her head drop. "I'll come up with one."

*Darren Shell*

Soon, Allen's truck rolled up to an odd intersection in the road. Four roads met here in the middle of a cemetery. His truck rolled off the main highway and into a short little gravel drive. His lights panned a large and foreboding log cabin. The ancient hand-hewn logs of Old Union Church were weathered gray with age. The windows had been boarded shut and locked. The doors were, in fact, padlocked from the outside, just as Allen had suggested. This two-story building looked even taller in the darkness of nightfall. Gravestones stood all around its foundation, crusted over with age and mold, much like the foundation of the building itself. The twisted old boards of the stairs out front were stained a rusty-red from the dripping of rain from the old metal roof. If the place wasn't haunted, it certainly felt like it could be.

David pulled his tools and strange gear from the truck.

"David…are you sure? This is breaking-and-entering. I don't want to go to jail." Molly really didn't want to go jail, and quite frankly, she didn't want to go into the building either.

"Where's your sense of adventure? New worlds are not found over calm seas!"

"It's not the sea I'm worried about. Are you just going to leave your truck parked out front?"

"We won't be here long enough to worry about someone seeing us. This won't take but a minute, and nobody uses this old road anyway."

Within seconds, Allen had popped the small screws of the door hasp from the jam. With a swift push, the door creaked open, revealing only darkness within. Particles of dust floated through the beam of Allen's flashlight, as he investigated the room.

A few old bench pews were casting shadows from the intruding light, and even a few old and tattered hymnals lie scattered across the nearly vacant floor. The dusty beams of the ceiling

*Graveyard Tour*

seemed abnormally close, and the walls of this large room seemed confining.

"Come on. We ain't got all night," said Allen, waving them in.

Before long, the contents of the truck and five pairs of eyes entered the room. Allen quickly took charge. "Set up the board, Scotty. Katie, light these candles." He scattered a number of strange, dry herbs around the Ouija board, as he leafed through the books he had brought. Before long, he had found the pages he sought, and began to recite incantations from the book, while the others looked on.

"Now," said Allen, "everybody sit cross-legged on the floor around the board. We need to maintain contact at all times. We will each place a hand on the Ouija pointer, and keep our other hand on the person next to us."

"Stop it, Scotty, not there," said Callie, sharply.

"Sorry…it slipped."

"Knock it off, you two, and pay attention," snapped Allen. "I'll do the talking. I'll call the name I've chosen first, then each of you will follow, in turn. Got it?"

All nodded into the darkness, looking all around them.

Allen began to chant and hum one of the spells from the book before him. "We five have gathered to summon names of old. We call their spirit forth from the dead. Can you hear us?"

The pointer of the Ouija board began to move. With the moving on the board, came a slight rumble in the floor. All five were surprised by the immediate response.

"Allen…I'm scared!" cried Molly.

*Darren Shell*

"Everybody keep in contact...don't let go! It's working." Allen continued to rap off certain quotes from the book, making strange gestures with his hands and arms. The glow of his flashlight grew pale. He called out again. "Can you hear us?"

The pointer of the Ouija board continued to move, spelling out a word. Each letter the pointer indicated was whispered among the five as it came to a stop. "Y...E...S"

"They hear us, David," cried Molly. "I'm scared!"

"We five call forth...Harry Springs."

The rumble in the floor grew louder.

"Allen, I'm scared..." mumbled Molly, with her eyes closed and her teeth clinched tightly together.

By now, all hands had left the pointer and were tightly grasping one another. As the boards beneath them shook, Allen motioned to Katie. With a timid and quiet voice, she squeaked out the name she had chosen.

"Cy McDonald."

The rumble in the floor increased.

"I'm scared, Allen," whispered Molly, her eyes swelling with tears.

Allen motioned to Callie, as Molly's fingernails pressed into his arm.

"Mary Copeland," said Callie.

Again, the rumble in the floor increased. A faint haze of light began to form above them.

Scotty needed no indication from Allen.

*Graveyard Tour*

"Little Joe Copeland!" he shouted aloud.

Molly shook from Scotty's words, and tears fell faster from her eyes. The floor continued to shake.

"We five," called Allen, "...also call..." He squeezed Molly's arm.

"I...I..."

Allen squeezed tighter.

"...I...umm..." Molly trembled head to toe and tears rolled down her face. She stammered and tried to speak.

Allen spoke again. "We five also call..."

Amid the flowing tears, Molly finally uttered one word.

"...Momma."

Allen's eyes grew wide, as he stared in disbelief.

By now, the rumble in the floor was shaking the Ouija board up and down, and the glowing light was increasing. A hum in the night sky was heard, and it was getting louder. The tin roof pounded... doors shook...the floor rattled louder and louder. Then, with one enormous flash of light, a deafening boom of sound pounded through the room like a bomb. The flash of light echoed from the center of the room like shock waves, knocking each of the five onto their backs.

And then...silence. Dead silence.

The thunderous explosion disappeared into the night sky, taking every ounce of light with it, and leaving five young teenagers nearly lifeless on the floor of Old Union Church.

# 11

**"Flight to Old Union"**

ne hour later.

"Hello?" David Shuler answered his cell phone, anticipating the call. He had heard his personal scanner announce an explosion in the Hilham area of western Overton County. He had already jumped in the truck and headed in that direction, when the call came.

"David?"

"Yeah, Jimmy, what's up?"

"You heard the scanner?"

"Of course, all hours of the night…I never miss a good story, if I can help it."

"I'm along the road to Old Union Church…about a half mile

before you get there. Stop and see me at my car. We need to talk."

"What have we got...kids playing pranks or something?"

"Yeah, Dave..." stammered Billy. "...yours."

\* \* \* \* \*

David's truck slid to a screeching halt in front of Jimmie Taylor's silver Honda Accord. The door quickly opened and David jumped out as he slid the shifter into park.

"Is she alright?"

"Well...she's stable."

"STABLE...what is that supposed to mean?" He raced back to his truck to jump in, but Jimmie caught him.

"Wait a minute, David. You need to know what's going on before you run down there. She's stable...I know that, alright? Listen to me...there's five kids broke into the old church. There was an explosion of some kind. All five are unconscious."

David raced toward the truck again.

"Damn it, Dave, listen to me. They think drugs are involved."

"What? My daughter? No way!"

"Think about it Dave...it sounds like a meth explosion. I don't know nothin' about it. But even if it ain't meth, something weird happened down there, and you better be ready for it when you go."

"My daughter isn't into meth. It's that simple."

"I guess she isn't into breaking-and-entering, either."

"Hold it right there, Jimmie. That's crap, and you know it!"

"Dave…prepare yourself, man. Five kids broke in that place, and Molly was one of 'em. We was kids once. Stuff happens, man. Just cool it and go to the hospital with your daughter. Me and Norrod will get your truck over to the hospital parking lot. I'll come in and see you when we get things wrapped up here. Go…be with her. She needs you…and there ain't no sense in being all mad about it."

David shook his head, "Thanks, Jimmie."

In a matter of a few minutes, David was sitting in the ambulance next to his daughter, wishing he could hear her voice.

# 12

**"A Friend in Need"**

"**Y**ou've been here for a day and a half. Why don't you go home and get some rest, hun?"

David's mother did her best to console her son. She had watched solemnly over the past few years as David delved deeper into his work, just trying to forget that tragic accident six years ago. Now he faced a similar situation…and she was certain that it, too, would take its toll. She had unselfishly watched and raised her granddaughter as many hours as she could. Many times she went to David, hoping to perk him up with a pep talk of some sort, yet it never happened. She just couldn't find the words, so things plodded along as usual. She now looked into her son's eyes and saw what mothers see.

"You've got to ease your mind, son."

"I don't know, Mom," he said with his head in his hands. " I don't know what to do." Tears began to fall from his eyes.

"I don't know all the answers, David. But I know that you need rest. You need to find peace somehow."

"I don't know how I could have missed this. Where the Hell was I, anyway? I was sitting at home, listening to the damn scanner… like a fool. Now look at her…" David stopped talking as the tears flowed.

"Go do something, David. Get some rest. Get your mind off of this, if only for a few hours."

There was a gentle rap on the door. "Hey, folks…any word?" It was Jimmie, from down at the sheriff's office. He had noticed that David had not yet moved his truck since it was delivered after the incident.

"Nothing yet, Jimmie, but thanks for stopping by. We're just here waiting."

"Say, could I get a word with you outside, David?"

"Sure."

The two stepped just down the hall and outside the building. Jimmie had a strange look of discomfort on his face.

"What's up, man?"

"We got a little problem."

"Man, we've been friends a long time. You can tell me straight up." David's eyes showed sincerity.

"The officers found some stuff in the old church."

"Jesus, not drugs, tell me."

"They found some strange herbs on the floor in the building. They didn't look like any drug I've ever seen, but the tox-test isn't back yet. I can't say what the stuff is."

"Was there anything else?"

"Yeah…" Jimmie paused again, as he swiped his foot over the ground, nervously. He stared down as he broke his silence. "They found some books on witchcraft, David."

"Witchcraft? I don't get it. My daughter? Witchcraft?"

"Uh huh…it gets worse, Dave. Aside from all the candles and Ouija board and herbs, there's one more trouble."

"Well?"

"Man, Dave, I hate to say this." Jimmie shook his head. "There was a whole file of your old stories in there, too. One of those stories is all about witchcraft, Dave. It talks about drug abuse…funky witchcraft crap. The police think you have something to do with these kids getting hurt…maybe even the drugs part."

"For Christ's sake, Jimmie…you know that's ridiculous. Never, NEVER, would I hurt any kid, and certainly not with drugs. No way."

"I know that, David. But regardless, I have to take you in for questioning. I got 'em to wait a day 'cause Molly was in here, but I need to take ya. It won't take long. Can your mom stay?"

"Man, Jimmie, that's my daughter in there."

"I know. Let's get this over with. I hate it as much as you. They're just doing their job. Every one of those kids in here has parents, and they want the truth, just like you. We need to clear your name. See if your mom can stay with Molly, so we can go."

\* \* \* \* \*

Two hours later, David and Jimmie sat on the steps of the Sheriff's Department. David had undergone a grueling interview with one of the officers.

"They're going to put me in jail, aren't they?"

"Well, not yet. But I don't know what to tell ya. It don't look good for the home team. What the heck were they doing out there?"

"I wish I knew, Jimmie. I don't know where this all came from. That damned report was never even published. I'm not some hoodoo chieftain sacrificing goats. It was a simple damn report, written by a bonehead, greenhorn reporter. I should have known better, I guess. Damn it!"

"You know them parents over there are gonna be lookin' for some reason…some answer for all of this. It ain't gonna fix itself."

"I don't know, Jimmie. I just don't know what to do. The only two things in life that I ever truly loved were those two girls. Now look at me. No matter how hard I work, stuff like this happens."

"None of that matters right now, Dave. What matters…is that little girl and you. Do what you will, Dave. But this deal ain't going away anytime soon. I suggest you put your mind to it."

"Man, this sucks. I really do appreciate the help, Jimmie. I know I don't listen so good, sometimes. Thanks for banging things into my head."

"Anytime, but I got work to do, Dude. Let me drop you off at the hospital."

Jimmie dropped off David at the door of the hospital and went on with his day. David stood and looked blankly at the hospital sign. A thousand thoughts were clouding his mind. Jimmie's words still echoed in his head. *What matters is that little girl...put your mind to it.* As those words sank in, he made a decision.

David dialed a number on his phone. "Hey, Mom, any word?"

"Not yet, dear. Where did you go?"

"Look, Mom, I need a few minutes to think. I'll tell you all about it when I get back. Can you stay a little longer?"

"Of course, Honey, but what's going on?"

"The police think I have something to do with all of this. I need to see if I can determine what really happened."

"I don't understand all this, David."

"Neither do I, Mom, but I'm gonna see what I can find out. I'll check in...and Mom...I love you."

"It's about time you said that. I thought you forgot who you were speaking to."

"Sorry, Mom. Call me if anything changes."

"Don't see how long you can be gone. I know how you are, David Lee."

"Talk soon, Mom...bye."

But even as David closed his cell phone, his heart began to sink. A sense of hopelessness came over him, and he wondered where he could start to unravel such a bizarre mystery. Witchcraft…Molly…drugs? None of it made sense. Why would she be at Old Union? All of his questions led to more, and for reasons unexplained, he decided to take a drive. At first, he slowly traveled the side streets of town, seeing more in his mind than what was really in front of him. But it wasn't long before his old truck rolled into the same gravel driveway as Allen's…two days earlier. For some reason, he felt the need to see that old church and cemetery. Maybe he just needed a church. He stepped from the truck and up onto the old steps of the abandoned church. He sat down on the steps and looked out over the cemetery.

The churchyard was cool and calm as he sat, viewing his surroundings. A pair of squirrels played in the side yard, barking and chirping back and forth. One tall fellow was walking through the cemetery in the distance, apparently visiting graves. A woodpecker tapped away at the rotting trunk of an old oak tree. There were no vehicles on the roads, and the only noises were that of the woodland creatures.

Despite the beautiful surroundings, David's heart sank even lower. All of the emotions of the past few days came flooding forth with all the *old* heartbreak he had been carrying. He talked out loud, between sobs, letting his mind go where it wanted. Amid the falling tears, he asked himself many questions.

"How could I be so stupid? It's no different than with Cindy." His mind flashed back to that awful night. He could almost feel the pain in his nose, and he definitely felt the pain in his heart. "I knew better than to drive so fast on that road. I knew better than to write that stupid report too. Stupid, stupid, stupid! I deserve this agony."

"Oh, I don't think so."

David had been so caught up in his troubles to notice the fellow from the cemetery walking up. His voice was startling, as he stepped closer.

*Graveyard Tour*

"What?" asked David.

"I don't think you deserve agony," said the man. His voice was very plain and comforting. He was a tall and slender black man of considerable age. His wide brimmed leather hat shadowed his face from the sun. "I am truly sorry to hear about your daughter's accident. She is a kind-hearted soul."

"Do I know you?"

"Why yes…yes…in a way," he said, with a nod of his head. "I am Harrison. I'd like to help…if I could."

"Well, Harrison," said David, "I wish you could help. Me and my daughter are having some real trouble. I don't know what happened." David let his head fall again, and he began to cry. "I just want to make her better."

"It don't work that way, David."

David raised his head. It had been years since someone had uttered those words to him…especially with his name attached. He was startled and a little angered by it. "What did you say?"

"It don't work that way, David…and you know it." The man paused and continued to look into David's bewildered eyes. "They brung a whole bunch of *bad* energy here, David…a whole bunch. You gotta fix it."

David became defensive. "Just how do you know so much about my daughter? I don't know no *Harrison*…and she doesn't either. Why do you know so much about these kids?"

"It's simple, David." The old man's ebony eyes sparkled in the mid day sun. "I was the first one they called."

# 13

**"A Voice from the Past"**

D avid's blood ran cold. "Who are you?"

"I told you…I am Harrison. I hope I can help you…and me."

David checked his pulse. He slapped his face. "Mother said I needed rest. I should have listened. Tired…just tired…yeah, that's it." He continued to talk out loud to himself, as the man beside him listened. "Got a lot on your mind, Dave. Take a deep breath. Ahhhh." He glanced back up at the man beside him.

"I'm still here, David," he said with a smile.

"How do you know me?"

"The friends of your daughter called my name. They were trying to call up the dead. Five young teenagers…calling up the dead! Bad idea, David. They might have gotten away with calling up one…but not so many. They're just kids. They were in way over their heads. Now you've got to help, David."

"How do you know my name?!!!!!" he shouted.

"David," he said calmly. "You know *all* of us."

"What the Hell are you talking about?"

"I think you know, David."

"I don't know you and it bothers me greatly that you know so much about my daughter and her friends!"

"Could we take a drive, David?"

"A drive? A drive? Harrison wants to take a drive…to help me." David shook his head in disbelief and anger. "Who are you, damn it?"

"David…I'm Harry Springs."

# 14

**"Balance"**

"Hhh…Harry?"

"Yes, David."

"*The* Harry?"

"Yep."

"You died! I know you did!"

"Yep."

*Graveyard Tour*

"But how? Harry Springs?…How the…?"

"Your daughter, David. She and her friends called my name first."

"My God!"

"Careful how you say that, David. That's not a good thing. What do ya say…let's take that drive."

"Drive…drive…yeah…think, Dave. Drive." He nervously tapped his foot on the step and tried to tune out the fellow next to him, shaking his head quietly with his eyes closed.

"You're gonna have to clear your head, David. We got lots to cover. I want you to think about the good of Molly. There ain't no other way around this mess. There's all this bad energy…bad, David. Them kids pulled up some bad, bad energy. Ain't nobody else gonna fix it but you. For every action…there's an equal and opposite reaction. Never forget that, David. You got to fix what they broke."

David was still trying to gather his senses. He kept looking at this man beside him. He was right there…large as life…Harry Springs. "You…you…" chattered David, "…can't be here."

"I can, David. I can. Now, let's take a drive."

"Do you want to drive?" asked David. "I don't feel up to it." He could not believe he even asked the question. He was certain that he'd left the deep end of the brain pool and sank beneath the surface. "I'm talking to a dead person. Brilliant, Dave. Toss him the keys!"

"I can't drive, David. I'm dead, you know."

"Right…right. You can talk…just not drive. Yeah, right. I'm with ya." David's head shook faintly, as he tried to believe what was happening.

"Don't get crazy on me, David. We have many stops. You ready?"

Strangely, David stood and walked to the truck. He was almost incoherent as the two slid into its seat. He continued to mumble as he walked...making observations along the way. He felt as if he was hallucinating all of the things he was experiencing. "Come along, Harry. Whatever, wherever...let's go."

"Why don't I talk, David, and you listen?"

"Seems like that's what we've been doing."

"Well, at least you are coming to your senses. Let's head toward Livingston. There are some people I want you to meet."

"Fine and dandy...Harry-o. I'm all yours."

"You really ain't dreaming, ya know?"

"Right...right," said David, with a laugh. "It don't work that way, Harry."

# 15

### "A Trip to Hidden Valley"

"Turn here," said Harry.

"I'm gonna stop and see Molly first."

"She's fine, David. They are all fine, so far. Turn left up here."

"I want to see how she is."

"You still don't get it, do you David?"

"I want to see my daughter!"

"Do you want to see her dead…or alive?"

"Don't talk that way! She's my daughter…she's all I have!"

"Then pay attention, David. I'm gonna lay it on the line for ya. We ain't drivin' around for fun. Them kids pulled up strong, strong forces. They pulled up evil and fear...they pulled up sadness, David. You don't just pull up dead people. It's all about energy...strong, strong energy. Somehow, some way, you got to find good from it. If you want to see your daughter alive again...you got to fix things up good, David. You got to find good in all of it. You got to balance the scales. Balance! Good and bad, David...you got to balance the scales."

David pulled off to the shoulder of the road and stared into the old man's eyes. "I'm trusting you, Harry. You better know what you're talking about."

"I ain't no tour guide, BOY! I'm a tryin' to help ya. I can't fix it for ya, or I'd a done-done it. This is *your* problem, boy. I'm just here 'cause them kids called me."

"I'm sorry, Harry. Let's go."

"Know this, boy...this ain't about witchcraft. This one's about YOU. If you want to fix her...you got to fix *you* first. Now...turn here. There's somebody up here you need to meet."

\* \* \* \*

One mile later, David's truck rolled to a stop near the top of one of the highest roads in the subdivision of Hidden Valley. The location overlooked much of the town of Livingston, and even a glimpse of the town square could be seen.

"Why are we here?" asked David.

"That's a tough question, David. I can tell you why I think we are here...but it is you who must decide for sure. I'll say it again... this is about YOU, David."

"Thanks...I need the pressure."

*Graveyard Tour*

"You need to fix your problem, don't ya?"

"Yeah, I guess. I'm sorry, Harry. Go ahead." By now, David was getting used to speaking Harry's name, and it almost seemed normal. After all, he looked real, talked real, and even acted real. And even though this all seemed like a dream, David just could not wake up...so he just played along.

"Look over this hill, David."

David's glance first missed the special slab stones just over the hill. He stared out over this pleasant valley town and admired the view. As his gaze returned to the foreground, he noticed them. "Holy cow...those are graves."

"That's Mr. Little Joe Copeland on the right."

"Who was he?"

"He was many things...a businessman...a farmer...even had a few shady deals going on...had a little moonshine deal cookin'." He paused and looked at the stone next to Joe's. "There on his left...that is Ms. Mary...his wife."

"I'm lost," said David.

"It's hard to just up and tell about a whole life, straight up, David. They were both many things. But I think you may remember more about them, if you try. Don't you remember the trial of Mary Copeland...and the murder of Ruth Daugherty?"

"Wow...yeah, I do. I remember Little Joe, too...built the courthouse after the Civil War. And...oh yeah...Mary Copeland. I wrote a story about her, but that was a long time ago."

"I was there that night, David. I was there the night Ruth came for Mary."

"What are you talking about?"

"Think back, David. You remember the story of when Mary died."

"Holy crap…you were the man *doctoring* her, weren't you? I never even considered that. Mrs. Copeland said that her Granny watched some man doctoring and praying…I should have guessed it."

"That was me…I was there. It was awful, David…I mean awful. Ruth had come for them both. She came for Little Joe, too. But I fought her…I fought that evil spirit of hers. I never seen such bitterness, no where. She fought me hard…I mean hard. In the end, I used the last possible bargaining tool I had. I had to tell her the only thing good to come of her death. I had to show her the good that came from her wretched and painful loss of life. But it was the last straw. It was the only way I had to save him…so I told her."

"What did you tell her?"

"It's complicated. You see…as I done said…every action has another one…an opposite. If you look hard enough…it is there. Look far enough down the line, and its there. Ms. Ruth just needed to be shown."

"Shown what?"

"If she hadn't have been killed, my family woulda been bought by different people, David. We were slaves. It's hard to say just how, but I wouldn't have had my upbringin'. I wouldn't a been taught what I was taught. I wouldn't a been able to help a whole bunch a people. I just wouldn't have been me, if she had of lived. It's sad…but true. A whole bunch of people would not have been helped. I finally convinced Ruth to spare Little Joe…but it wasn't no easy task. It took all I had."

"I think I see how you did what you did. I just don't know how it pertains to me."

"Me either, boy, but I hope you do when we get done."

"Done with what, Harry?"

"You got lots a questions, boy. Try listening some more. Never know what you might take in."

"Sorry, Harry. I just have questions."

"Boy…you was born with two ears…and one mouth. Understand?"

"I'm getting there, Harry. I'm getting there."

"Good. Get in the truck."

**"Joe and Mary"**

"Turn here."

"For somebody who can't drive, you sure make a good back seat driver."

"Two ears…one mouth, David."

"Gotcha."

By now, the two had left Hidden Valley and drove back the way they came. They had gotten back on Highway 85 and traveled a couple of miles west.

"Are we going back to Old Union?"

"Nope. Pull over in this little drive."

David's truck rolled to a stop just a few feet off of the south side of the highway. They were looking out over a small valley dotted with small brush and briars. In the distance, on a knoll, was a run-down log building. Its weathered logs were gray with age, and what few wooden shake shingles still resting on its roof were trying to fall. As David scanned his surroundings, he noticed two people standing in the field in front of him. They were side by side, and looking directly at David. Although they were many yards away, he could tell that it was a man and woman standing hand in hand.

"I don't think we're supposed to be here. They're looking at us like we might be trespassers."

"Oh, I think we're supposed to be here. That's Little Joe and Mary."

"Holy crap…that's creepy. What do they want?"

"I told you, David. I ain't no tour guide. This is all on you. I just know they are here, just like me. And somehow, you got to figger out why."

"Then, I'll talk to them."

"It don't work that way, David."

"Man, you've *got* to get a new catch phrase."

"Two ears, David. Now, it's like this. In life, some people can reach the spirit world…they can communicate. Some just can't. I always could. It's just like that in the spiritual world. They are there…they just can't really communicate like me. I always could see both sides. Most folks can't."

"Hummm." David scratched his head, trying to make sense of it all. "Okay, tour guide. What do I do here?"

"I don't know...I'm done here. Ready to go?"

David looked out across the field again. Little Joe and Mary stood patiently hand in hand. The look on their faces was solemn. "They don't look happy, Harry."

"They ain't happy, boy. They been called back. No matter what happened in life, David...ain't none of us happy to be called back. None of us."

"How many people did those kids call back?"

"Five."

"Wow...five? Something tells me we've got more driving to do."

"Yep. We're headin' east, boy."

"Alright, let's do it."

"Cy"

David's truck wound eastward through the hills on Highway 52. "Are we going to Alpine?"

"Not quite. Take a right up here."

The two turned right and traveled down a twisted side road. It wasn't long before Harry was pointing to a small, fenced-in plot of land just off the road.

"Pull over here."

David started to pull into a small field.

"Don't pull in. Just stay on the road. Don't turn off the engine."

"But I don't see anything."

"You will. This is the McDonald Cemetery."

"I don't remember any McDonalds."

"Oh yeah, you do, David. Remember Cy?"

"Cy McDonald...hummm. Josiah...the Marshall after the Civil War?"

"Yep."

"He was killed by the moonshiners...buried in a cave north of town, wasn't he, Harry?"

"Yep. Let's go."

"They found his bones years after he died."

"Yep. Let's go."

"But, I haven't seen anything, yet, Harry. Shouldn't we get out? Let's wait a minute."

"Put the truck in gear, David."

"I always felt bad for that family...never knowing what happened to him."

"Drive, David!"

At that moment, a large rock crashed onto the hood of the truck. Then, a scream was heard. Out of the corner of his eye, David could see a figure rushing toward the truck. Before he could get the truck in gear, the body of a man slammed into the side of the pickup, pounding on the hood with both fists and screaming at the top of his lungs.

David slammed the truck in gear and sped off, leaving the figure in a cloud of dust and exhaust, his arms waving furiously.

"Why didn't you tell me that was going to happen?"

"Two ears, David…two ears."

"What's his problem?"

"It's like I said, David. Ain't none of us too happy to be here. Cy died a cruel and painful death. Bringin' him back here is like… well…what you're fixin' to face."

"What do I have to face, Harry?"

"You got to face number five, David…and old Cy is gonna look like your play pal after that."

# 18

**"Facing Cindy"**

The two were just rolling into town, when Harry gave his command.

"Turn here."

*Graveyard Tour*

David's heart sank. He knew this road well. Memorial Gardens is a beautiful little cemetery on the edge of Livingston. David pulled into this driveway nearly every week of his life since the winter of 2000. Cindy was buried here, and David knew every step of every grave nearby hers. It was a place of great sorrow for him, and just pulling in the driveway grieved his heart. He choked back tears as they entered.

"There are a lot of people buried here, Harry."

"Bunches. Stop right here."

David swallowed a lump in his throat. "I don't want to stop here…I can't." Tears fell from his cheek, as anguish poured from his heart. "I'm not stopping," he sobbed, as he looked at Harry. The truck continued to roll slowly forward, as David fought his emotions.

Harry looked out the front window of the truck. "You got no choice, boy. We're stopping."

David turned his eyes back to the road ahead. He slammed on the brakes in horror.

"MY GOD!" he cried. "Cindy…my God…Cindy."

\* \* \* \* \*

David shook from head to toe. He cried uncontrollably, as he sat behind the wheel of the truck. He slowly slid the shifter into park and looked over at Harry.

"I can't face her," he said, his face awash in tears.

"Get out of the truck, David. It is time to fix the problem."

David's shoulders sank, as he stared out the window in total disbelief. There she stood…large as life…just as beautiful as ever.

Cindy...his Cindy. "I can't face her, Harry. I can't do it." He rested his forehead on the steering wheel as the tears continued to fall.

"You got to, David. She's here for a reason. You got to face her."

He reluctantly pulled the door handle of the truck and stepped outside onto legs of jelly. He managed to place one foot in front of the other long enough to collapse in front of her.

"I'm so sorry...so very, very sorry. I don't know what to do, Cindy. I miss you...I love you so much. I'm lost without you. I'm sorry. I'm so, so sorry."

"Stand up, David."

He was so startled by her voice, that his crying stopped, and he knelt breathless in front her. He was too caught up in his sorrow to think that she might actually speak.

"Stand up, David," she said again.

He quickly scrambled to his feet, tears falling again from his cheeks.

"In every life, David, there is a time to laugh...and a time to cry. You have cried for me far too long. Stop blaming yourself for my death. It was an accident. It was no more your fault than mine. You lost me by accident...you are losing your child by choice."

"No! She's the greatest thing in the world to me. I just feel horrible...I...I took her mother from her."

"God took her mother from her...not you, David. God."

"What am I supposed to do?"

"Move on, David. It's that simple. Move on. Until you get

over our past, you will never have a future. And *our* daughter will suffer. For me…and for her, David…move on." With that, Cindy turned to walk away.

"Don't leave me…please don't leave. I lost you once…don't make me lose you again."

"You've only lost me once, David. You don't have me back now. What you have is your daughter…but you *must* let go. Find the good, David…find the good in this whole thing. And above all… move on…*and be there for **our** daughter.*"

With that, she turned and disappeared, leaving David standing heart-broken and dejected, wishing he could go along.

# 19

**"Letting Go"**

"Get in the truck, David."

"Huh?" David had been so caught up in the moment that he had forgotten Harry was in the passenger seat of his old truck.

"Time to go, David. There are five of us that want to go home. I think you've inconvenienced us enough."

David tried to gather himself enough to go. He wiped tears from his face and took a number of deep breaths. It was all just too much to take in. And Cindy…that memory was the tooth that tore at every fiber of his being. He desperately wanted her to stay…wanted her back in his life. She was right there…why couldn't she stay? Why couldn't things be like they were when she handled everything, and he just loved her for doing it. Since that December day, his life had been lonely…empty. He had life all around him…yet he was an

*Graveyard Tour*

empty shell of self pity.

"You're not losing her again, David. That's a done deal. What matters now...is the one that's left. Don't lose that one, David. Cindy said *our child.* Remember that."

"Okay," he said, reluctantly. "Let's go where ever." He dragged his feet to the truck and slid into its seat. "Where to, tour guide?" he said, letting his head fall back against the back glass of the cab of the truck.

"Old Union, of course."

\* \* \* \* \*

By the time David's truck entered the driveway of the Old Union Church, the evening sun had set and the landscape had darkened into a dusky, shadowy terrain. A light mist drifted between headstones of the cemetery, and the temperature had dropped a number of degrees.

"What are we going to do, Harry?"

"That's a tough question, David. I'm taking *us* home. *You*...on the other hand...that's a whole different deal. First...you got to *let* us go. And then...if you really want to help them kids over there... find the good, David. Find the good. Ain't nobody but you can do it."

By now, the old man had stepped from the truck and walked out into the cemetery. David followed him into the darkness of the graveyard, watching closely as the old man chanted and talked out loud. He would sometimes pause at a headstone and say a few words. He even asked questions of some of them and patiently waited for answers. He was in a world all his own...and yet, it had many, many voices echoing through it. His presence seemed to mingle all things...just sort of spun everything together in a fantastic and beautiful display. Light followed him where ever his footsteps plodded. Energy abounded all around him, and life seemed to be richened by it. He was a rainbow among clouds...seemingly ageless...timeless. If there ever was a bridge between what we know and what we don't...it was Harry Springs. His compassion... his energy...his aura was like none before him, and it shined like the beaming stars above him. The darkness of Old Union Cemetery was enlightened by his spirit, and all the landscape was illuminated by his rich presence. He was Harry Springs...*the* Harry Springs. And life pulsated through his lifeless body...summoning four other souls to follow.

"But Harry...are you going?"

"We will be, David. But we can't go just yet."

"I don't understand, Harry."

"It's all about you, David. You have to *let* us go. We came as one...we go as one. What you do after we leave...that's the real question. Will you let us go, David?"

The cool mists of the cemetery began to swirl around Harry. Strange figures began to take form. Swirling mists of light and raw energy formed before David's eyes, and he wept with its beauty. A man and woman appeared at Harry's side. Little Joe and Mary's solemn faces longed to leave this world.

Soon, the angry and snarling figure of Cy McDonald took form, swirling in unrest and dismay. Harry appeared to be holding him back.

And then came the heart-breaker for David. Cindy slowly and sweetly appeared before him, swirling in the mist. She was not near the others. She was right in front of David, her head tilted with compassion. Her eyes were as soft and gentle as any memory David cherished. Tenderly, she smiled and spoke.

"You are holding us back, David. It is time to let go. You must

*Graveyard Tour*

let me go. I cannot come back…and you must not come with me. You have *our* daughter. *OURS!* In her…there is some of me…some of me, David. Cherish her. Love her. *LOVE OUR DAUGHTER.* Through her…some of me lives. Some of me lives, David. Let me go. Let us all go…and move on."

David dropped to his knees. His head fell back on his shoulders. Tears rolled. "I love you so much…"

"Then let me go, David. Move on with your life. Savor what you have before it is gone. I am happy, David…and I want you to be."

"But I miss you so much."

"I know, David. But it is time to let go. I am happy. Be happy, David."

Amid his tears, he looked into the eyes of all before him. Little Joe and Mary stared back…tears also falling from their eyes. Cy growled in anger…impatiently waiting to leave. Harry smiled, knowingly, as he looked at Cindy. And Cindy…ah, Cindy…her eyes warmed the souls of all who were present. Her energy was as strong as any among them, and it radiated from her like the warmth of the sun. "Let us go, David. It's time."

Amid the sorrow…amid the deepest of heart-felt anguish David had ever known…he gave in. In that one decisive moment in his life…in that one heart-breaking, life-changing occurrence…David spoke the hardest words he had ever spoken.

"Good bye, Cindy."

"Go see her, David," said Cindy, smiling. "She is waiting for you. Go see her…go see *us.*"

The air began to move around them. The mists that had drawn these five here together were now drawing them away. The light that had surrounded them all was now fading. Faster and faster the winds blew, creating a spinning funnel cloud of light and splendor. There was a hissing rumble in the air that grew and grew. Slowly, the cloud lifted from the ground…swirling, hissing. With one enormous implosion, the light and wind collapsed in on itself, disappearing into the night with a clap of silence. The cemetery of Old Union became dead silent.

\* \* \* \* \*

David slowly and methodically walked to his truck. He turned the key in the ignition and pulled out onto the highway. Aside from the turmoil of the past two days, he had not slept since the night before it all started. He was lethargic and nearly incoherent. His body steered his truck to the hospital, as his mind drifted into the unconscious. Upon his arrival, he walked straight to Molly's bedside and took a seat. Oblivious to his mother at the foot of the bed, David took Molly's hand in his and placed his head on the edge of the bed. Within seconds, he was fast asleep.

**"Feeling Better"**

"David…David?" called his mother.

"What…what?" David lifted his head from the bed and shook himself awake. "I'm sorry…I must have drifted off."

"Drifted off? I was afraid you were going to fall out of the chair. You've been sleeping for eight hours."

"Sorry, Mom. I'm beat. I should have come sooner. I'm sorry I haven't relieved you, so you can rest. I know you need it. I'll be okay now."

"Where did you go?"

David scratched his head and pondered what he had dreamt, and what he had actually lived. Bits and pieces were filtering back into his head, and he remembered most of his day before. "I went to Old Union…to find some answers."

"Did you find them?"

"I think so," he said with a yawn. "I found many things, Mom. I have a better understanding now."

"You're talking out of your head, Hun."

"I'm alright, Mom. She's the one we need to worry about," he said, looking at Molly. "Why don't you go home, Mom. Get some rest."

"I guess I could go home awhile. I think I'll check on the other kids first."

"Good idea, Mom…thanks. Let me know if there's any change in them."

"I'll be back later on."

David glanced back at Molly. He still held her hand after all night. Her hand was limp, but warm, and David just could not let go. It was his lifeline to her, and she was the only thing on his mind. He raised her hand to his lips and kissed the back of it, gently breathing words upon her skin.

"Things are going to change, Honey. As God as my witness…I will be there when you need me…when I should be. Just please… please…come back to me. I love you so much."

"I know, Daddy."

Her voice shook him to full attention. "Molly! Thank God in heaven. You're awake!"

"I missed you, Daddy."

"I missed you, Honey." He pressed her hand even further into his face and continued to kiss it, with tears falling on her fingers.

"I'm sorry, Daddy. We shouldn't have been at the old church. I know better."

"Don't worry about that now. We have plenty of time for that."

"Daddy...I mean it. I knew better. I'm scared of what we did. I'm scared!"

"Don't you worry about it, Honey. I think I have that covered."

"Covered?"

"Honey...I know who you kids called up. I'm gonna fix it. I promise. One way or another...I'm gonna fix it."

"Daddy, what we did was ugly...it was awful."

"I know. I don't like it any more than you. I caused this mess with that stupid old report. I'm gonna fix it all, one way or another."

"There's something else, Daddy."

"What is it?"

"I...I saw..."

David squeezed her hand and kissed it again.

"I saw Momma."

"Ohhh," sighed David, as a look of anguish engulfed his face. "Ohhhh."

"She was right there at the foot of the bed, Daddy." Molly paused and looked longingly at her father beside the bed. "She's happy, Daddy…she's happy. She let me know she's okay. And I feel better about her, Daddy. I feel better."

"I know, Honey…I know." David paused and looked into her eyes. "I saw her, too. I feel better…I feel better."

\* \* \* \* \*

Inside the halls of Livingston Regional Hospital, five teenagers awakened to loving families. Five young souls looked at the world through different eyes, and one local reporter made a promise to himself…and to his only child. And when he made that promise… he meant it. And for the first time in his life, David Shuler did not back away from his family to go to work. He backed away from his job…to work on family.

# 21

"Walking Off the Turkey"

Before the weekend arrived, all five Livingston Academy students were back in class with many stories to tell. All faced charges of breaking-and-entering but were cleared of all drug charges. The tox-tests done on the herbs brought by Allen had all came back negative for illegal substances. Despite the public ridicule endured by Allen and his friends, all five recovered from their apparent ailments after the ordeal. Molly had explained her actions of that night many times over, and still felt a pang of guilt for not facing the peer pressure with the strength and magnitude she normally showed. But she was able to move on, learning a valuable lesson.

David seemed strengthened by the whole thing. He seemed happier than in recent years and spent much more time doing the family things he'd missed out on over the years. He reflected on that strange night in his life many times, and remembered the words of Harry…and of course, Cindy. Even though the kids had all recovered and David felt better about himself, he couldn't shake those words from Harry. *Gotta find the good, David. Ain't nobody else gonna do it.* He resolved to keep searching for *the good,* whatever that might be.

\* \* \* \* \*

A few weeks had now passed since the incident. Most everyone had forgotten the little trouble out at Old Union. The town was full of Christmas lights and Thanksgiving was in the air.

David sat completely reclined in the chair at his parents' house. He was full of Thanksgiving turkey and dressing and had fallen completely asleep in front of the television.

"Dad…Dad?"

"Huh, what?"

"Just wondered if we could change the channel."

"Hey…I'm watching the ballgame," David said, wiping his eyes.

"You're watching the inside of your eyelids."

"You sure know how to interrupt a good nap. I was just dozing a little."

"Dozing? Bulldozing, maybe. I think you were crumbling the

ceiling plaster with your snoring."

"Is there something you wanted, nuisance?"

"How about we walk off some of that turkey?"

"Ugh. That isn't exactly what I had planned for my afternoon."

"Now Dad...pleaseeee."

"Alright, alright. Give me a minute."

"Do you want to go, Grandma...Grandpa?" Molly asked.

"Too cold for me, Dear," said her grandma. "Maybe next time."

"Urm, uh, mmm," mumbled Grandpa, as he snuggled back into the chair.

"I guess it's just you and me, Pop."

"I'm up, already. Grab a coat, kid. That wind is chilly."

Despite David's lack of enthusiasm for the walk, the sun did feel good to him, and he enjoyed talking away with his not-so-little girl and walking Livingston's side streets. Many years had passed since the two could just walk and talk and be happy together. They had walked for twenty or thirty minutes when Molly brought up the topic the two had chosen to avoid.

"I've been meaning to ask you something, Dad."

"What's that, Hun?"

"When I was in the hospital, and we talked about seeing Momma, you said that you thought you had things handled. What did you mean by that?"

"That's a tough question, Hun. I saw a bunch of strange things that evening…your mother being one of them. I saw all of them, dear. I saw them all."

"You saw the people we called?"

"Yeah…all five of them."

"How? Did you use witchcraft? Did you send them back?"

"No, I didn't use witchcraft," he said with a scowl. "I think you know better than that. There were no funky chants or incantations. It was mostly about your mother…and how I needed to let her go. It was the hardest thing I ever did…letting go."

"I'm sorry, Daddy."

"Don't be, honey. I love you so much, and what happened that night is over and done. I watched those souls disappear into thin air. I've never seen anything like it in my life."

"How did you make them leave?"

"Harry did all the work. Plus, I think they were all more than ready to go."

Molly tried to imagine how that night could have unfolded, and what her father must have endured. The mere thought of looking into Harry Springs' eyes gave her chills.

"What was Harry like?" she asked.

"Harry Springs is a neat fellow."

"I'll bet he is. Did you get to talk with him much?"

"Well, no. He pretty much did the talking. He was a remarkable fella, though. I was amazed by him...by his energy."

"Was there anything else special about him...about that night?"

"Just one thing that tugs on my mind."

"And what's that?"

"Harry kept saying that I had to find the good from all this. He said that nobody else was going to do it. I had to find the good... me."

"I'll help you, Dad. If nobody else is going to do it, then I'll help."

"Thanks, sweetheart, but I don't know what to look for. I don't know how long this stuff takes. I just plain don't know."

"Then I bet it will come to us. We'll cross that bridge when we come to it. I bet someday, down the road, it will come to us. There will eventually be something good come of all of this. We just don't know how long it will take."

"I suppose you are right, my dear. Maybe it will seem simple someday."

The two continued to walk around downtown Livingston. They had made several laps around the courthouse, thinking of old Harry Springs and chatting about his interesting past. The court square was decorated nicely with Christmas ornaments, and the blustery winter's day seemed perfect for an after-Thanksgiving walk. Molly hummed a little Christmas tune as they walked.

The courthouse had a number of large red bows attached to its brickwork, and some of its high windows had fogged over in the cold winter atmosphere.

"Look, Dad. Isn't that cute? Some little kid has written her name in the fog on the windows. I used to do that." She pointed to the upper windows of the courthouse.

"I know…I washed the windows in the house after you boogered them all up."

"Sorry."

"It's always something with you, kid. I don't know why I keep ya."

"You'd miss me," she chirped with a smile.

"Yeah…maybe," he grumbled with a smile, giving her a playful push.

As the two walked a little further, David turned around and looked back at the courthouse. "Walk back here a minute."

"What is it?"

"Some of those windows have black panels behind them to keep the light out of the room up there. A kid couldn't get to the window to write on it."

"Yeah, that's weird," she said, as she looked up at the windows. "And wouldn't the words be backward," she asked. "…you know… written from inside, the words would look backward to us, wouldn't they?"

"Well, yeah…I guess it would. And how does anyone get inside the upper courthouse on Thanksgiving? The doors are locked."

They both gave one another a questioning glance and looked again at the upper windows.

"That's really weird," said David.

*Graveyard Tour*

Molly read each name aloud that was on each of the upper panes of glass. "Mary...Joe...Zollicoffer. I don't get it."

David was deep in thought, as he stared at the hand-drawn words on the glass. "It doesn't make sense to me either. How did those letters get there?"

"Beats me," said Molly. "The only Zollicoffer I ever heard of was the Civil War General...the one they named the camp after."

"What camp?"

"Well...Camp Zollicoffer...named after General Zollicoffer, where they trained the Confederate soldiers during the Civil War. They turned it into a park later, with a golf course and lake. It closed eventually. It's nothing more than cruddy pasture now. The old clubhouse cabin is still there, I guess, but that's about it...we just studied it in history class a year or two ago."

"Was it near here?"

"Oh yeah. It's just outside of town, on the Hilham Highway. Why?"

"I don't know. Something just seems strange about it. I guess it's my over active imagination. Oh well, I'm starting to get cold... and that chair is calling for me...and the ballgame. I'm about ready for some pie, too."

"Yeah...we've gotten way too much exercise for mere turkey, alone."

"Agreed. Let's head to Grandma's."

"Agreed...and Dad?"

"Yeah."

"Thanks for walking with me."

"No sweat, dear. I'm not missing any more of these little family things. I've already missed far too much of you. Thanks for prying me out of the chair."

Molly smiled from ear to ear. "No sweat, Pop."

As the Christmas lights flickered off and on in downtown Livingston, the two skipped off to Grandma's for pie, living life like the rest of the world should, year 'round.

# 22

**"Morning Jog"**

The morning sun had just peered over the hills and into the valley of Livingston on the busiest shopping day of the year. Molly Shuler still felt full from the pie and ice cream overdose at her grandparents' Thanksgiving get-together. She had slipped out of the house much earlier than usual this morning, leaving her father snoring loudly within the confines of his room.

By most measurable means, Molly was a late sleeper, but today had all the makings of a fun day for her. She woke early and gathered her things for a quick jog across town. Many of her friends were getting together to begin work on the Christmas parade float they had planned for a number of weeks. This was to be the year that the juniors of Livingston Academy were to trounce their senior classmates in the parade float competition. Molly would normally have been happy to sleep away her morning after Thanksgiving, but today her school pride had warmed her for an early morning jog. She left a tidy little note for her father and closed the door quietly behind her.

The chilly morning air stifled any sleepiness left in her brain as she stepped to the curb. She took a couple of long stretches before beginning her mile-long journey, tucking her ears neatly beneath her wool cap and watching her breath drift off into the frosty air.

She quickly covered the two-block distance to the square before turning toward Allen's house. Allen's father had donated the use of his garage to the junior class for the building of their float. The weather had been unseasonably cold, slowing its completion, and Allen wasted no time securing his father's warm building to complete their work and keep it secret and safe until the unveiling next week. In all honesty, it wasn't a particularly spectacular float, but the students were quite proud of it and wanted it safe from prying senior eyes. Molly made her turn on the square, pondering the float in her head.

As she jogged along near the courthouse walls, she glanced at the upper windows, half expecting to see tiny finger print markings upon them. Even though the windows showed no signs of fingerprints, the markings from the day before danced around in her head, as she bounced along her path. She paused at the corner, still jogging in place. At once, her mind flashed back to a comment made by Scotty on that fateful night over a month ago. She stopped flat-footed and turned slowly, looking back at the courthouse.

*"Dad always said that guy left treasure in the courthouse... left clues or somethin'. Dad's been all through it and ain't found nothin'."*

Scotty's words echoed in her head. She also had one more voice filtering into her mind. It was her father's...repeating Harry's.

*"Find the good, David. Find the good."*

It's hard to say what was really on her mind right then. Even she didn't know for certain. But one thing was a definite...she felt something in her heart...and Molly promised herself that she would never question her heart after that scary night at Old Union.

*Note to self...think on courthouse incident.*

"Molly," shouted Katie, from across the square. "On your way to Allen's?"

"Yeah, care to join me?"

"Oh, I don't know," she jousted, jogging in place. "...can you keep up?"

The two immediately jumped into a run, leaving the courthouse square in a bitter-cold blanket of frost. The tall and colorful brick walls of the courthouse seemed to enjoy the display...and waited patiently for Molly and family to think some more.

# 23

**"Scotty's Clue"**

David rolled out of bed just after Molly left the house. He began his usual morning rituals of turning on both the coffee pot and the computer. In a matter of minutes, both were prepared and ready for him. He would normally type in his access code and begin work on one of his many stories at the newspaper. But today, something was on his mind.

"Let's see what my friends at Google know about old Zollicoffer." He typed in a few key words. *Camp Zollicoffer, Livingston, TN.*

The first heading on the screen was for a website of a local writer who did stories about historical places and people in the surrounding area. Her articles appeared every week in another newspaper in Livingston, *The Overton County News. Josephine's Journal* was a treasure trove of local history, and sure enough, she had studied the old Zollicoffer camp and had written up a wonderful little article about it. David clicked on the icon and began to read.

There indeed had been a camp at the site during the Civil War. The article went into further detail about the park that was built in later years, telling of the small lake and golf course that once graced the grounds. It wasn't until the pictures came up that David got a cold chill in his spine. In the center of his screen was a photo of the old golf course club house. It was the same log cabin that he and Harry had visited over a month before, where Little Joe and Mary had been seen, standing in the field. This photo sparked a number of thoughts in David's mind. *Why did we go there? Why would Joe and Mary be standing there? Mary, Joe, Zollicoffer. There must be a connection.*

David quickly grabbed the telephone and dialed a number. "Hello, Emily?"

"Yes."

"Hey, this is David Shuler. Have you got a minute?"

"Sure, David, what can I do for you?"

"I've been reading your Journal entry about the old Zollicoffer Camp. Do you know who owns that property now?"

"I know two of the three. It was divided into tracts when it sold years ago. There is a retired woman that owns the middle tract, and the one closest to the road is owned by a local family. I can't think of their name...I have it written down somewhere. Wait a minute... you know them. Their little girl got messed up in that trouble out at Old Un---Oops! Sorry, I forgot yours was involved, too."

"That's alright, Emily. I hope we're past all that now."

"Well anyway, it's that little Callie girl's family that owns it."

"I didn't know that. I know the family fairly well. I just didn't know where they lived."

"What have you got going on at Zollicoffer, anyway?"

"Well, I don't know for sure. I just want to go take a look at the place. I may give them a call. I sure appreciate all the info, Emily. Thanks a bunch."

"Anytime, David. Let me know if you find something...makes for a good follow-up story."

"Will do, Emily, thanks again."

In a matter of seconds, David had his shoes on and was out the door. He jumped in his pickup and drove over to Allen's garage. A number of cars were parked out front along the road, as David rolled to a stop. As he suspected, a large group of juniors was busy attaching paper and letters to their float entry. It didn't take long to find Molly and Callie gluing garland to the float.

"Hey, Dad. What are you doing here?"

"I just came to ask Callie a question."

"Go ahead, Mr. Shuler...shoot."

"I just wondered if your parents might show me around your property. I'd like to take a look at the old log building from the park."

"Daddy is at home today. He'd take time to show you around, I'm sure."

"It wouldn't bother your mother, would it?"

"I don't think so...she doesn't get far from the couch these days."

*Graveyard Tour*

"Alright," said David, compassionately.

"I'm going too, Dad."

"Why?"

"This is about the courthouse deal, isn't it?"

"Well, I think so, but I don't know for sure."

"Let's take a break, Callie. Let's both go."

Although Callie had no idea what they were talking about, all three piled into David's truck and drove over to Callie's house. The two filled Callie in on the details on the way. They passed the old campsite before turning into Callie's driveway. David looked out over the pasture, half expecting to see Little Joe and Mary still standing where he saw them before. But, he saw no one. Frost still lingered here and there in the shadows of the field, and the old log club house building could be seen, resting forgotten in the far distance.

As David's truck rolled to a stop in Callie's meager little gravel driveway, she spoke up. "Daddy's not here. His truck is gone. He always parks in the drive."

"Should we come back later?" asked Molly.

"No. It's fine, I just need to let Momma know we're here. You can get out if you want. I'll meet you in the field in a few minutes." Callie bounced in through the front door and disappeared.

David and Molly began a stroll into the field. Molly watched closely, as her father seemed to be retracing steps…as if he had been here before.

"You were here, weren't you?" she asked. "You were here, back in October."

"I was here," he said, distracted.

"Hey, wait up," chirped Callie, as she left the front porch. It wasn't long before she met up with the two of them. "What are we looking for, again?"

"Shush," said Molly. "He's thinking."

David continued to walk out across the pasture, gazing now and again toward the road to get a reference of where he stood. He eventually came to a spot in the pasture and stood, thinking long and hard. Molly could no longer hold her silence.

"What are you doing?"

"Harry showed me this place. We stood back over near the road. Mary Copeland and Little Joe stood right here while we talked and watched them."

"They were both right here?" Both girls stood cold in their tracks, with chills running through them. Callie wore an especially strange look on her face.

"Right here," said David. "Mary and Joe…right here at Zollicoffer. Mary, Joe, Zollicoffer. Make sense?"

"Not really."

"We are finding the good, ladies…finding the good. At least I hope so."

All three stood staring at the ground, wondering why they could have been led to this spot. They continued to look all around as well, as if searching for some other clue. Finally Callie spoke up.

"What *good* could possibly be in this old pasture?"

"There has been a lot of history here, Callie. It is hard to say

*Graveyard Tour*

what could be on these grounds." David paused and rubbed his chin in deep thought. He began to think out loud.

"We are standing in the middle of this little valley...the old lake bottom of the park from the 1930's. But picture this place even before that. This smooth lake bottom wasn't always so smooth. Imagine this place as the Confederate training camp of the 1860's. This place would not have been so flat then. There would have been tents and crudely-built buildings...there would have been obstacle courses...even holes. Imagine those dug-out fox holes used to train soldiers. They were probably here for years...even after the war. Little Joe was still alive then, and maybe even Mary. They only lived a couple of ridges over from here. Would they have had some sort of reason to be here? I have heard that Little Joe was into moonshine, but I don't see how that could fit in."

"What about the moonshine?" asked Molly.

"I don't know...would the soldiers have bought moonshine?" asked David.

"They would have used some for medicinal purposes...but I don't think very much, if that," commented Callie.

"Would they have had time to drink any?" asked David.

"I doubt it...not much," said Molly. "They were soldiers."

"I agree. It wouldn't have been very much," said David. 'They may have sipped some, but not bunches. I don't think that would have much to do with it."

"Then why are we here?" asked Callie.

"Let's think back to those fox holes," said David. "I don't know if that's how soldiers were trained back then. It may have been more about hand-to-hand combat than fox holes."

"Fox holes were WWI, weren't they?" asked Callie.

"I have no idea, Callie…all I want to know is what happened right here."

"Then, what's another point of view?" she asked.

David thought a minute. "Think about this…yeah…think about it this way. This was public property. This was a government training grounds for soldiers. Even after the war…most everyone would expect it to remain public property. Let's say you had some money…illegal money. Let's say you had MOONSHINE money. Let's say you've spent all you can spend without being caught. What are you going to do with your money? After the war, looters and guerillas were stealing and burning and pillaging everything in sight. That's what happened with the courthouse…they burned it to the ground. So…what would you do with your money? You'd bury it. You'd bury it just as soon as you could get it in the ground. If the Union Federalists didn't take it from you, the damned guerillas would pry it from your dead fingers." David paused with a smile. "You'd bury your money as fast as your shovel would dig."

"But why here?" asked Molly.

"Think about it! If you bury money on your property, it is considered yours. If somebody found it, they'd either steal it, or turn you in. But if it were found by an official…maybe even a Union official…it would be yours to stand accountable for. You'd be jailed…or hanged. This was the Civil War…it wasn't a happy place."

Both girls struggled to keep up with David's story. They looked to him as he continued to talk. "If someone found money buried on public property, who's to say where it came from? No matter who found it where, it was gone. But at least if it was found on government property, the original owner (Joe) could not be tied to it. Little Joe would not have been held responsible for it, if it had been found in this stretch of property. Plus…just maybe…there were some large holes already dug here. Maybe Joe was in a hurry to get his money buried. Maybe it was easier to bury it in a hole that was already dug and ready to be filled in. Maybe this was the fastest and safest place in town to bury things. No one ever came here after the war...the war was over. Out of sight...out of mind. Maybe his money is still here!"

"But where?" asked Callie.

"Right here, girls," said David. "Right here."

"Why?" asked Callie.

"This is where Little Joe and Mary were standing when I saw them."

"You saw them right here?" asked Callie.

"He saw all of them, Callie..." said Molly. "I just never told you."

"I saw them all, Callie. Those five people you kids called...I saw them. I saw Joe and Mary standing right here...right here."

Callie looked at the two of them with an astonished gaze. "You've seen them, too? I was afraid to say anything."

David and Molly returned the same questioning glance. "You've seen Joe and Mary?" asked David.

"Yeah...both of them...right here."

The three all stood bewildered, their minds awash with confusion.

Callie shook her head slightly and gave a quiet laugh. "You know...that might explain the shovel."

"The shovel?" asked Molly and David.

"Yeah, the shovel. When I saw them…Joe was holding a shovel. He had it extended toward me…showing it to me."

David smiled at Callie. "Callie, my dear…I think we are about to find *the good.*"

# 24

**"Finding Good"**

"I don't suppose you have a shovel, Callie?"

"Daddy has two."

"Run and get them for us. We have some digging to do."

Callie quickly returned and the crew began to dig all around the spot that the Copelands had been seen. After over an hour of digging, they had a large hole dug in the soft soil of the old lake bed.

"Do you think we are digging in the right place?" asked Molly.

*Darren Shell*

"I don't know," said David, stretching his back and arms. "I thought we would have found something by now." By now, all three were filthy from head to toe, and their hands were beginning to become blistered.

"I think I'm done, Dad," said Molly, sitting down on the edge of the hole they'd dug. "I'm beat."

David and Callie both sat down as well and wiped the sweat from their brows. Despite the cold winter weather, the three had shoveled enough to work up a sweat.

"My dad is going to think we're nuts, you know," laughed Callie.

"Yeah," said David. "We look pretty ridiculous. I suppose we can give up. It was worth a shot, I guess." By now, the morning sun had aged well into the late afternoon. None of these shovelers had bothered checking the time as they sweated over the open hole.

"I don't want to give up yet," said Molly, who was already continuing her shoveling. "I think everything we discussed makes sense. I have a few more shovels-full left in me."

"Just because it makes sense doesn't mean there is buried treasure in this hole," remarked David, taking a few more shovels of dirt from the ground.

"Ugh," grunted Molly, with a shake of her hands. "I've hit rock. I guess we are at the bottom of the hole."

"I'm deeper than that over here. Are you sure?" asked David.

Molly pushed her shovel back into the soil. Thud...solid rock. She moved over a foot or so and pushed again. Thud...rock again. Once more she moved and pressed her shovel into the clay. This time, it slid straight into the soil. "Maybe we haven't found the bottom."

*Graveyard Tour*

By now, David had jumped from his side of the hole, and crawled over near Molly. He, too, dug around the large rock in the dirt. In a matter of a few minutes, the three began to see a distinct shape emerging from the soil. It was in the shape of a cylinder, about two feet tall and nearly as wide. Whatever was buried in this dirt was no rock. It had been placed here…and a very long time ago, at that.

A few more shovels of soil were removed, and the three could finally make out what the object was. To their surprise, an old stoneware crock sat in the bottom of their hole…where it had apparently been for many years. They dusted off its heavy lid and looked at the remains of what was once its wire-bale retainer. The old wire had rusted into oblivion, and the lid sat comfortably in its original position. A large number 10 was stenciled into the outside of the crock, indicating it was produced to house ten gallons of liquid. David gave out a laugh. "If there's ten gallons of moonshine in here, I'm going to be very disappointed."

The three stared at the old crock in front of them, itching with anticipation, yet wary of its possible contents. What could be worth burying one hundred and fifty years ago? Could it be money… guns…deeds to property? Could it really be moonshine in this old crock? All three sat nervous and excited.

"Well?" asked Molly. "Are we just going to look at it, or what?"

David smiled and took a deep breath. "Alright…here goes." He took the edge of his shovel and gently pried at the seam of the lid. It immediately gave a grinding and hollow echo from inside. David slid his fingers beneath the edge of the lid and gave a strong tug. The lid slid off to the side, revealing the crocks contents.

"Holy Crap," said Callie, "what is all that?"

David gave her a knowing smile. "I think it's your mother's Christmas gift from God."

# 25

**"Cousin Ronald"**

The phone on Ronald Dishman's desk rang. He had just settled into his office chair after an early shower. "Honey," he called aloud. "Could you get that? I'm on line with the historical society."

Ringggg.

"Honey, could you get that?"

Ringggg.

"Don't bother," he grumbled. "I got it." He picked up the receiver while staring at his computer screen. "Hello?"

*Graveyard Tour*

"Ronald...this is David. You got a minute?"

"Well, at the minute, I'm kinda busy."

"Let me rephrase that. Get your butt out of your pajamas and answer your door. I'll be in your driveway in five minutes."

Ronald raised his eyes from his computer screen to the clock on the wall. "It's 8 o'clock...this better be good."

The three had taken their sweet time in carting the crock from the field to the truck. The sheer weight of its contents had made the job lengthy and tiresome. After a long conversation with Callie's parents, and the better portion of an extra large pizza, the time had gotten quite late.

"Dude...you'll be glad I came to see ya," said David, almost grinning through the phone.

Just as David had suggested, his knock rapped upon Ronald's door in a little over five minutes. Ronald stood in the door in his robe and wooly slippers. "You really know how to get on my nerves, David."

"I also know how to strike them too!" David walked into Ronald's foyer with the two girls following. Molly chuckled at Ronald's fuzzy slippers and continued to walk. "Don't laugh," he chided to Molly. "Did you arrive by broom...or just stew some hog's wart and eye-of-toad?"

"You're not nice, Cousin Ronald," said Molly, with a smile.

"And you are in my house at eight o'clock, Witch Hazel. And who are you, young lady?" he asked, looking at Callie, "...evil sidekick?"

"Good Witch of the North," she replied, with a crafty grin.

"As I stated earlier, fine folk in my living room..." said Ronald, "...it's late. This better be good."

"Oh Ronald," began David, "...as *I* stated earlier...I know how to strike your cords. Tell me what you think of this." David pulled a silver coin from his front blue jean pocket. He almost tossed it into the air for effect, but thought better of it. He ran his thumb across its face and handed it to Ronald.

Ronald took the coin from him and examined it. "Looks like a Seated-Liberty half dollar. Nice condition. Good clean coin. What's the big deal? It's probably worth fifty to one hundred bucks, tops."

"Look at the back."

Ronald flipped the coin and examined the star-spangled bird on the back. "It's the standard eagle that's on all of them. So?"

"Read the words, Ronald...the words."

Ronald glanced back at the coin in his palm. David watched Ronald's lips move as he whispered the words inscribed on the reverse side of the coin. "Confederate States of America." His hands began to tremble. "A real Confederate fifty-cent piece! I have never held one!" He read the words again. "Confederate States of America...wow."

"So what do you think its worth?" asked David.

Ronald continued to stare at the coin in disbelief. "Can you document where you got it?" he asked. "You don't just find these every day. Can you prove it's real?"

"I believe we can," he replied.

"The last one I saw was on EBay. It wasn't this nice. It sold for $1,900.00."

*Graveyard Tour*

"Wow!" commented David, with a huge grin. "How many could we sell?"

"How many you got?" he asked, his jaw nearly hitting the floor.

David gave a wry smile. "Oh…about two hundred pounds of them."

# 26

**"A Quiet Solution"**

Ronald paced the floor in his wooly slippers. By now, the clock had struck 11, and he had heard the story told by David and each of the girls. Although the facts seemed to jive, it all just seemed a little too much. "So we got ghosts in our little town…got confederate moonshine money…got a big hole out at Zollicoffer Park. I don't like the sound of all of this."

"What do you mean, Ronald," asked David.

"I don't like the sound of any of it, David. Think about it. If word gets out on this…every treasure hunter in the country is going to be digging holes in Callie's yard. People will come unglued. The Civil War junkies will go through the roof! We need to think about this."

*Graveyard Tour*

Ronald had a point. As a reporter, David immediately understood the consequences of what could happen by letting this all get out to the press. There was yet another thought to consider, also…and Ronald was quick to point it out. "Think on this, too. There haven't been twenty of those coins change hands in over a year. They just don't come up for sale. Imagine dumping hundreds of them on the market at once. You'll flood the market…straight up. Plus…I think the value might come down on them with that many re-entering the market. We need to sit on these awhile. You know…let a few go to market each year."

David gave a dejected look. "We were hoping to give a little cheer to Callie's mom with this news. I really thought we were finding the good in this whole deal. These all came from their property…they technically belong to Callie's family…and they could certainly use the money right away. You know her mother, right Ronald?"

"Yeah…I think I follow you now. We need speed…and, of course, quiet. Let me think on this a minute. There's an answer here…let me think."

"You know, Ronald…there's another little problem, too."

"What's that."

"I wonder what lawsuits could come from family members of soldiers…previous property owners…Civil War buffs. We might be in law suits for years."

"I think I have your solution, David. Chill out a minute. I need to make a phone call." Ronald disappeared into another room of the house and picked up the phone. He quickly dialed a memorized number into the phone. His muffled voice could still be faintly heard.

"Hello, Jim. It's me, Ronald Dish-…yes…yes, I know it's late. I have an opportunity for you. I think it would be worth your while.

Could you come over? Yeah, I really think you'll wish you had, if you don't. Yes, yes...it will be. Trust me."

Ronald reentered the room and sat down on the sofa. "Let me think a minute. There's an answer here, someplace...I can feel it."

In a matter of minutes, a tiny BMW convertible pulled into Ronald's drive. Ronald walked to the door and glanced out into the night sky. "Stay here. I'll be back in a moment." He pulled the door shut behind him and walked to the car.

Molly peered out the window into the drive. "Callie...that looks like Allen's dad's car. Do you think it might be him?"

"I can't tell. The windows are too dark."

It seemed that Ronald had been in the drive an eternity when he finally reentered his living room. The little BMW quickly made its getaway into the darkness. Ronald looked at David. "I think we can work things out. I had to let him borrow the first coin...to check it out. He can be trusted. He loves history, just like me...loves it. It would be worth quite a lot to him to own these particular coins. He wants the crock, too. He doesn't even want it washed. The coins are valuable on the market...and even more valuable to someone local who wants a piece of real local history. Bring it all to me when I call. We will work out the details in a couple of days."

"Can he be trusted, Ronald?"

Ronald laughed out loud. "He's a history buff and a very good friend. These coins are small potatoes to him, David. Livingston is Livingston because of his family. Don't worry. They are safer now than when you arrived. They are safe, my friend."

"Then we will talk soon, Ronald. Thanks for your help."

"You're welcome, David. Always glad to help...only much earlier in the day next time. I'm going to bed, if you people would just kindly leave my living room."

David gave him a warm smile. "Thanks for your help, Ronald. You're the man." As David spoke these words, he slipped another coin from his pocket and into Ronald's hand. "For my history guru…thanks again."

"Don't mention it, David," he said, sheepishly. "…ever."

# 27

**"Completing the Circle"**

Three weeks later.

David's truck pulled into the driveway of the Cash Cemetery. The late morning sun had warmed the frost in the yard, and the grass shined with silvery dew. He stepped out of the truck and slowly walked toward the back of the cemetery. He paused in front of a familiar headstone. He knelt and wiped his hand over the words inscribed on it. "I've come for a visit, Harry."

A voice came from over David's shoulder. "And I have been waiting patiently."

*Graveyard Tour*

David stood and turned with a knowing smile. "I thought I might find you here."

"And so you have. It is good to see you, David. You have done well, my friend."

David's smile continued to radiate. "It is good to see you, Harry."

"I believe you have found the good, David."

"I think we did, too. I'm so happy for Callie's family. They've had a hard battle. I am glad that something good truly could come from this whole mess. Her mother should recover quite well the doctors tell us."

"Do you think you've balanced the scales?"

"I think so. I think I finally understand how this whole thing works. But I'm a little foggy on something."

"I'm listening."

"This whole thing is kind of a circle. We are all kind of connected someway. First, you said that because of Mary Copeland, Ruth Daugherty died…somehow changing your upbringing. In turn, your upbringing helped nurture your gift of foresight…your gift of healing. Your gift saved Little Joe's life that night when Ruth came for Mary and him. You said you talked her out of taking Joe. That saved his life. One action led to the other."

Harry nodded his head, smiling.

"So, Little Joe lived long enough to get big in the moonshine business. So big, in fact, that it eventually took Cy McDonald's life. Now, if my thinking cap is on straight, it would tell me that there must be something good that came out of his death…but I can't imagine what good could have come from such a horrible tragedy.

*Darren Shell*

He was a great sheriff."

"I think," said Harry, "that I can shed some light on that for ya." Harry scratched his head and searched for the proper words.

"When Cy went missing, there was a big search party. People from all over the county were knocking on doors and asking questions to try to find him. Cy's son found himself knocking on doors he would never have knocked on. A young lady answered one of them doors and looked into the eyes of her future husband. That's how they met. Are ya still with me, David?"

"Yes. I think so."

"Them people met because of that one terrible action. They got married, David, and they had a son that became a lawyer…the same lawyer that held the bag of bones that belonged to his grandfather, Cy, seventy years earlier."

"Wow. That's amazing." David pondered the possibilities of it all.

"There's a little something else, too, David."

"What's that?"

"That lawyer…he had family, of course. Three generations later, a pretty little blonde granddaughter was born into his family. And she, David…she grew up and fell in love with a dashing young reporter in Livingston, Tennessee."

David closed his eyes, as a tear slid down his nose. "Cindy."

"Yep."

David's head rolled back on his shoulders, and he took a deep breath. "I had no idea, Harry…no idea." He took a few steps though the cemetery, letting the information soak in. He had not seen the

*Graveyard Tour*

full circle of events until just now. He paced back and forth in the little cemetery, just letting his mind catch up to speed. He finally walked back to Harry and looked into his eyes.

"I guess that leads us right back here to you and me, Harry."

"I reckon it does."

"That's why you're still here, isn't it?"

"I reckon it is."

"Then what is it that I can do for you, Harry? How can I complete the circle? What positive influence could I possibly offer Harry Springs?"

Harry gave a warm and knowing smile. "I wish the world didn't think I was some crazy fella in Livingston, years ago. I wish they knew the full story, David. I wish they all knew what really happened. Me and my girls…we built those walls that still stand. We built the foundations that still hold houses. Our belief in the Lord kept us strong. That is what I really want people to know. That's how David Shuler could help Harry Springs. Tell my story, David." He paused and smiled warmly. "Tell my story."

# 28

**"Novel Idea"**

ne year later…

The door to the Livingston Enterprise swung open, and in popped two young ladies. "Hi, Dad."

"Hi, ladies. How are you?"

"Good."

"Got my pictures?"

"Here you go, Mr. Shuler," said Callie, rummaging through her purse.

"Thanks, Callie. Do you want to cover tonight's game, too? I'll need center court photos of both teams. Interested?"

*Graveyard Tour*

"Yeah, no problem."

"How's your mother doing?"

"Oh, she's great. She hasn't worn her back brace in almost a month. The doctors have been impressed."

"Excellent! Happy to hear it."

"Any word back from the publisher, Dad?" asked Molly.

"Yeah, looks like they're going with it. They talk like they could have the book on the shelves in a few months."

"Great, Dad. What did you decide to call it?"

"Well, I think we're gonna call it *The Graveyard Tour*."

"Fantastic, Dad. Me and Callie decided we want a cut of the royalties."

David wore a grin from ear to ear. "It don't work that way, ladies…it don't work that way."

**The End**

**Author's Review**

A large amount of the happenings in this story are of historical record. You can find them in the history books and newspaper articles from years past. But, by and large, this story is fiction. *All* ghost stories are difficult to prove otherwise. I have taken the liberty of changing a few names to protect the innocent, and moved certain minor timelines in the essence of telling a good story. These were inevitable. But over all, I have tried to remain historically correct wherever possible and remain true to Livingston, Tennessee. For Livingston is a forward thinking city, with its roots in the past. It neither lingers in the doldrums of the past, nor races blindly into the future. It merely moves forward with grace and beauty.

For the record, I don't think Cousin Ronald wears fuzzy slippers. I just think that's funny. Sorry, Dude.

In closing, I will say that I walk the streets of Livingston much like David Shuler. I stare at its architecture. I sit on the wonderful old walls Harry built. I sip fruit tea at The Apple Dish. And I sometimes think I can see ol' Harry Springs walking quietly amid the weathered headstones of its cemeteries. I've visited his headstone many times, hoping he'd walk up from behind and chat. I'd just love to meet that old fellow…but it don't work that way, Darren.

Thank you, Livingston.

D. S.

Copies of Mala Terry's courthouse sketch can be purchased at the Overton County Heritage Museum.

"Angel of Good and Evil"

Copies of this and other prints by Darren Shell can be obtained by visiting his website"

*dalehollowgravedigger.com*

## Other Books by the Author

### *Stories From Dale Hollow*
This historical look at Dale Hollow Lake is full of wonderful pictures and short stories about the lake and the Obey River Valley.

### *The Gravedigger's Guide to Dale Hollow*
This non-fictional work maps all of the relocated gravesites from the Dale Hollow Lake Project. It also contains many interesting stories of folklore and places of interest on the lake.

### *The Prophesy Rhymes of Tal Kator*
This short fantasy novel tells of the whimsical ways of a group of leafy creatures and their troubles with wizards, trolls, and old monks. Fun and entertaining.

### *The Prophesy Rhymes of Tolk's Tomb*
This fictional sequel leads readers further into the lives of the monks of Cobblestone Abbey and their turmoil with the king.

### *The Old Lady of the Lake*
This fantastic fictional book of short stories chronicles life in the Obey River Valley, and begins with the famous ghost story of the moving of the graves during the making of Dale Hollow Lake. This is Shell's first book, and contains many historical facts along with the fun and entertaining ghost tale.

### *Graveyard Tour*
This fictional ghost tale of good versus evil chronicles much of the history of Livingston, Tennessee. It's chilling storyline tells of one young reporter's struggle to understand the strange and bizarre occurrences at Livingston's most haunted location...Old Union Church. Meet ghosts of Livingston's past on this treasure hunt/mystery novel.

## About the Author

Darren Shell has authored many works in fiction as well as compilations of historical nonfiction books about his hometown of Livingston, TN, and Dale Hollow Lake. Shell was raised on the lake and was compelled to record the lake's rich history, especially those concerning the creation of this man-made lake and its prior residents that were forced to move from their beloved homes. At the time of this writing, he still offers historical tours and ghost walks in Livingston. He resides with his wife in Allons, TN, near family and the lake that he loves. They are blessed with two children and eight grandchildren.

Made in the USA
Columbia, SC
28 February 2023